SPIN THE DAMN BOTTLE

ALL THE GAMES WE PLAY BOOK TWO

MAY SAGE

EMM DARCY

Spin the Damn Bottle

All The Games We Play # 2

By Emm Darcy | May Sage

May Sage © 2022

Edited by Theresa Schultz and Nicole Zoltak

WARNING

To my readers, this is book two! You enjoyed book one enough to click on this one and I should thank you for that. But when I finished writing *Spin the Damn Bottle*, I figured I should also warn you.

If you read *I Fucking Dare You* and thought something along the lines of "It's a little bit much for me, I'm not so sure about this...but May Sage usually has my back so I'm going to trust that she'll deliver something similar to her other titles," please close the book. I love you, I value your support and your trust, and I absolutely have May Sage contemporary titles planned for you later! But this book is not for you.

Emm Darcy isn't May Sage. I created this pen to have the freedom to explore a completely different vibe.

Book one was a little toe in the pool. *Spin the Damn Bottle* cannonballs in.

It's sexy, it's nasty, it's doesn't conform to usual relationship norms, and it gets dark in places.

Jason is unapologetically selfish, and will never take no for an answer. He's not even close to a hero. His love is more akin to obsession and his absolute control over Nadia would make you stage an intervention if you knew the poor girl.

The thing is? It's fiction, and Nadia fucking loves their dirty games.

The list of content warnings is a mile long, but in short, if you don't like gray romance, this series isn't for you.

CHAPTER ONE

I f given the luxury of choice, I recommend a third-degree burn. At least it kills the nerve endings, so the pain is limited in the affected areas. First and second-degree burns aren't as gracious. *Everything* hurts, my hands most of all. The only thing that seems to help is when Jason takes them in his and kisses them.

Then the deafening sting is joined by an itch that makes me want to peel my skin off.

After one week of boredom and suffering, I beg my doctors to let me out, but they're reluctant to do so, even though I'm out of danger and they don't seem to do much. It's only after my uncle pulls some strings and promises to hire a nurse to check on me daily that they send me home with creams and pain killers.

That's when I set out to let Jason go.

I should have done it earlier. Like my mother, he came to visit me every day at the hospital—all day at first, then

I made him go back to school, but he drove back to the city after practice and stayed long past the posted visiting hours.

Every day, I told myself I should end it. Every day, I chickened out. I needed him, and I chose to be selfish for a little while.

I can't put it off any longer, so I tell him I'm done on my release day, an hour before my parents are due to pick me up.

It's over. I could deal with what he's done to me—his calculated cruelty didn't break me. I don't mind his deviance, and I knew all along he wasn't the vanilla, missionary position type. I mean, I saw him and his friend going at it with a girl in the locker room last year, for Christ's sake.

And I found it hot.

None of that scares me, but I'd be insane to accept the danger that comes with being part of his life.

"No."

I should have expected that exact answer, but I didn't. "You can't say no," I shoot back, reasonably. "I just told you I want to..." I can't even say break up with him. He never asked me out in the first place. I'm not his girl-friend. "I don't want to spend time with you anymore. It's my choice." I'm proud to hear myself sound stern and decisive.

Too bad Jason Alden has never been one to respect my choices. Too bad I don't particularly respect this choice either.

He runs his hand over the bandaged, leather skin of my palms, ever so softly, and I wish I didn't love that touch as much as I do. "If you actually meant it, if you didn't want me, I'd consider your opinion," he lies. "But you're just afraid. With good reason. These scars are there *because* of me. You should want to run."

Jason has always been unfairly perfect compared to me, and that was before burn scars covered fifteen percent of my body. They run along my right side, from my neck down to my hips, and on the hands I used to try to get out of the furnace. My hair had to be cut to my shoulders, and is completely shaved in places. I have an undercut now. My mother turned up with her trusty hairstylist to fix the mess the doctors made in the process of saving my life.

My new style is cute, edgy, maybe even trendy, but I still don't recognize myself in the mirror.

"I won't let you," he tells me softly. "You can fight me as much as you like. You know I quite enjoy when you do. How often does it work out on your favor, though?"

Never.

When I hated his guts and did my best to push back against him, he made my life a living hell at Cross and Roses. It only improved when I started to accept the inevitable: he has more power than I ever did or will. As his enemy, I'm less than nothing. When I'm by his side, people leave me alone.

And yet I know what I need to do, for *both* of our sakes. "Your world and mine don't mix, Jace. Someone's pissed about you and me. The moment you stopped terrorizing me, they killed a cat. A week later, we hung out at your club, and they escalated to arson. I'm not going to take that risk again. Whoever is responsible for the fire was trying to *kill me*, you get that? It's not a game."

Jason's lips curl up, though his gray eyes remain cold as ice. "Everything is a game, cupcake. They've just upped the stakes. They tried to claim your life. Now I'm going to destroy theirs."

I should have known he'd turn this into a challenge. It's personal to him. By attempting to take my life, my mysterious attackers pissed on his territory. Good for him, but I refuse to be a prize in a deadly tug-of-war. "Fine. Get on with your destroying. Just leave me out of it."

His steely gaze sets on me and I recognize his look. I saw it at the start of the school year—after challenging him and his friends for terrorizing Judith by the locker room—and many times since. I'd like to think I'm no longer afraid of it, but I know better than to believe Jason's done hurting me. He'll never be safe. If our opinions align perfectly, all is well. If they don't, I'm as likely to suffer his wrath as any of his enemies. We might have reached a truce, but only because he's getting what he wants out of me.

"You're mine, Nadia," he says slowly, patiently, as though he's trying to make a very dumb puppy learn something. "Mine. And the entire world will know it. You, first of all."

Seeing the familiar, heated glint flashing through his eyes, I half expect him to take me right there on the hospital bed, heedless of the unlocked doors or the constant coming and goings of nurses and doctors. My parents are due to arrive any minute, but I might just have let him, too, if only to feel him again, one last time. His touch is a weakness I've never understood. When he was my enemy, I couldn't resist it. Now, every caress is addictive.

We've only had sex once, and that was in a public venue, before the eyes of dozens of his friends. When I didn't even question him, letting him take me, I began to understand how deep his hold on me is. Is there anything I'd say no to, when he has the ability to make me lose all sense?

He does something worse than fucking me. Jason turns on his heels without another word and walks out, leaving me wanting and oh so confused.

It's great, I tell myself. Exactly what I wanted.

Why does his retreat taste like ashes?

CHAPTER TWO

I spend two weeks at home, and it's fine. I'm a little
bored during the day, though my mother stays with
me. She babbles a lot of time, but I don't mind.
Every afternoon, when they finish school, my friends
pop by.

Evie, Gabrielle, Spencer, and Harper have been a
constant in my life for years, and even after my uncle
enrolled me in Cross and Roses, I made a point of seeing
them as much as I could during weekends and holidays.

Tara and Olivia, my work buddies, pop by after their
day shifts at my father's restaurant.

I missed my old crew so badly at Cross, and now I see
them almost every day. I tell myself I'm glad to have them
in my life again. Truth is, I want to return to school, badly.
The same school I've always hated and wanted to escape
just in September.

Sophia's barely talking to me, so I can't even lie to myself by pretending I miss her. I don't.

But I miss *him*.

You're mine, Nadia.

I groan in frustration. He didn't mean it, because he would have fought more to change my mind if he did. Instead, he disappeared.

Willow Brown has either volunteered or been assigned to pass on notes and homework to me, though we don't share every class. As a scholarship kid at Cross, she can't exactly afford to say no when the faculty ask her for a favor, so I'm guessing they made her do it. We're friendly enough, but I can't imagine her willingly reaching out to several of my classmates to put together all of my assignments on top of her already busy schedule. She has her own classes, several tutoring sessions, work after school, and she told me about her little brother—a toddler she and her sister take care of.

Mr. Green finally moved on from *Romeo and Juliet* to *Wuthering Heights*. I smile when I see that, guessing Cain's not impressed with another romance—though arguably, this one is even worse than the first. He protested studying "romantic crap" at the start of the year. Green might have set out to annoy him.

I shoot him a message, reading the neat, color-coded notes Willow passed along.

Me: **Another kissing book! You must be delighted.**

He replies almost immediately, though he must be in history class.

Cain: **Green is the fucking worst. You just know that perv picks love stories so he can get girls wet when he reads that crap.**

I roll my eyes.

Me: **He's a teacher.**

Cain: **He's a hot blooded 23 year old male. Trust me, he gets his pecker wet.**

I grimace, though objectively I have to admit that Mr. Green is far too young and attractive for a teacher. Still, I've never seen him do anything inappropriate in class. I wish Cain's dirty mind hadn't put that thought in my head, because I'll have a hard time meeting my favorite teacher's eyes when I get back now.

I've only put my phone down for a second when I get a series of notifications.

Rowan: **Are you texting Cain?**

Rowan: **You're totally texting Cain. He's grinning smugly and showing his phone to Jason.**

Rowan: **Come on, spill. What happened with Jason???**

To my surprise, three of the kings of my school have taken to texting me, most of them daily. Maverick only messaged me once, a strange one wanting to know my favorite color—paler purples, like lilac or lavender. After answering him, I asked why he cared, but I got radio silence. The guy's weird.

Rowan mostly sends me pictures of Anakin Skywalker

burned to a crisp, and keeps begging me not to turn to the dark side. Cain's my most faithful correspondent—I can count on a message every day. He sends me tons of selfies that happen to include Jason—on the football field, at parties on the lake, outside the courtyard.

I don't get any messages from Jason himself, so he must have heard me, whatever he said.

Mine. And the entire world will know it. You, first of all.

Right. What a load of bullshit. I suppose he got what he wanted from me. I'm not particularly great at sex, so he must have been bored enough to move on.

I decide I don't feel any particular way about it.

My doctor finally agrees to let me go back to school at the end of the week, only it's the start of the holidays, so I won't get to return for another couple of weeks. At least my mother is less freaked, so I can go to the Christmas market, have brunch with Uncle Lucius and Lucas, and go ice skating in the park. Which is a terrible idea, really. I fall and my sore body aches so much I almost pass out, but I don't tell anyone about my pain level hiking up to an eleven out of ten, lest they lock me up for another month.

We spend Christmas Day as we always do in my family: my parents and I visit Lucas and Uncle Lucius's house in the Hamptons. They also have a penthouse in the city, but I think they purposely drag us out to the holiday home so that my father doesn't run back to his restaurant in the middle of the day. It's open, unlike everything else in the city, but my mother makes him take that one day off.

We exchange silly presents—the family tradition is to never spend more than fifty bucks per person. I think Uncle Lucius implemented it to make sure Dad doesn't feel left out, when he's unable to match his budget. My haul includes a pretty sketchbook, paintbrushes, a new phone case, and a makeup bag that surely pushed past the fifty, but Dad doesn't need to know that, and no one else cares.

I'm surprised, after we've all unwrapped our presents, when Lucas tosses me a small square box wrapped in black silky paper, and adorned with a red bow.

He's waited until we're alone, cleaning up the dishes, which is in itself rather odd. "What's that?"

"None of my business, that's what it is. Unless he's a problem. Then it will very much become my business." He holds my gaze meaningfully, and my heart skips a beat.

I know who the package is from.

Part of me wants to run to my bedroom and open it alone, away from Lucas's curious eyes, but I shrug nonchalantly and open the box. Inside, rests a platinum band adorned with a letter studded in diamonds. *H*. Which could be odd, given the fact that my name is Nadia Reyes. Not an *H* to be seen. But I've seen that letter before, on top of a digital contract I had to sign. It's also plastered on the front of an imposing Upper East Side building, belonging to one of the world's most exclusive clubs. The Heritage.

There's no note in sight, but I don't need one to be certain of the provenance.

I need to murder the kaleidoscope of butterflies suddenly dancing inside me for good.

On New Year's Eve, exactly at midnight, I finally hear from him.

Jason: **Be ready.**

That's it, just two words.

I don't reply, but I analyze them over and over again over the next few days. By the time school starts again, I'm uneasy. Whatever he's planning? I doubt I'm anywhere near prepared for Jason Alden.

CHAPTER THREE

I smile at the girl seated opposite me in the limo like I'm not meticulously planning to break her.

It's not about her. The poor thing doesn't have any inkling as to why her life is about to become a living nightmare. She, as far as she's concerned, has done nothing wrong.

The fucking idiot is elated I'm taking her to the New Year's Eve party thrown by the Heritage. She knows about us—her family's worked for us for two generations. Her cousin even became a blossom a couple of years ago, joining our ranks. Marie Vaughn hopes to follow in her footsteps.

"You have the longest legs." I tilt my head. "I'd love to see more of them."

She's quick to lift the fake velvet up, while sending me a pout that's supposed to be sexy, I guess. My dick is completely comatose. Thankfully, I'm not alone, or I'd fuck up this operation.

Cain stops kissing Melina long enough to say, "Spread them for me, darling. I want to see your lovely little cunt."

Marie's too happy to oblige. She would have made a good addition to the Heritage, eager to please in order to get what she wants out of life. She's tall, tanned, athletic and not entirely stupid, though her choices belie that. In another world, she would have ended up attending an Ivy League school of her choosing, opening her own art gallery, eventually marrying one of us.

Too bad for her, she chose the wrong side.

I don't plan on punishing anyone who pushed Nadia when I asked them to. They were good little sycophants, following my directives without question. But I'd informed the school of a cease-fire, and she fucked with Nadia nonetheless, in a big way. The only way that truly bothered her. She destroyed Nadia's art.

That meant one thing for someone like Marie—she's a follower. She wouldn't dare move a toe out of line without permission, especially against *me*. Someone told her to keep bullying Nadia. Someone she believes has enough power to protect her.

Even from me.

I don't know why she was dumb enough to accept my invitation today. Maybe Nadia's absence empowered her. It is useful in many ways. I could start to lay the foundation for the necessary changes at Cross. With Nadia by my side, my reach would have been limited. I understand men who prefer to make their way into the world without a partner for that reason alone. Making people believe they have a chance of earning a place by my side has always been useful. America works on fantasies, on daydreams. Women behave more predictably if they're vying for the ultimate prize: the wealthiest, most powerful guy around. The king.

Marie's one among thousands of hopeful souls. She and the others like her never had a chance. If it weren't for Nadia, I would have followed the predictable course, fucking around for a while before marrying Yuki Moore as my parents want me to. And then fucking around while being married to Yuki, with her and behind her back. Our arrangement would have been cold and emotionless, but it would have worked out. Most parents I know are bound in similar dynamics.

Andrey Moore isn't stupid. He knows his daughter's smart, efficient, and cunning. He also knows no one will take her seriously at the head of his empire, because she happens to have a cunt rather than a cock. Yuki needs a suitable husband to appear at her arm, although she'll likely be the head of Moore and Moore all the same. I understand it, and I was willing to play the part, because joining our legacies seemed like a logical step.

Except I'd rather not be a miserable asshole for the rest of my life, and I know that a marriage to Yuki leads to no emotional support. A cold, sterile partner, not dissimilar to myself, would mean sleeping alone every night, never bothering to have a conversation about my day. I'd be richer, so there's that. Yuki wouldn't care how many pussies I fuck every night. She'd require I sire a couple of kids and then ignore the rest of my affairs so long as I extend the same courtesy. Hell, she'd even let me keep Nadia as a mistress if I pushed.

I don't want that. I don't want to become my father. He might be fulfilled in many ways, but he can't hide what I see in his eyes.

Nothing but ice. The same cold void that has inhabited my heart since my twin brother's death.

The one thing stronger than the practicality of a legacy match is the law of attraction. I've only heard of a handful of instances where men and women in my shoes broke a betrothal arranged by parents to unify filthy rich bloodlines. It's always because one of the parties was obsessed with someone else. Obsessed enough to turn their back on billions of dollars.

Nadia Reyes moved me at my worst, when I was staring at the void and wanting nothing more than to jump. I *need* her. She doesn't make me happy as such. It's not an emotion I can sustain for long. She makes me feel, which is better. With her, I'm almost human.

I was pragmatic enough to test her, check whether she could handle pressure. I knew very little about her at the start of the fall, and a weak spirit can't possibly survive in our world. Nor can a prudish one. If she'd fail, I would have still kept her, but I would have had to take precautions. Hide her, lock her away. Marry Yuki and never let the world discover my vulnerability. I don't think it'll come to that. Nadia is perfect for me. Soft enough to bend to my rule, proud enough to resist everyone else.

Until the fire, that is.

Her limit literally is murder attempts, and I can respect that. She's ready to give me everything else. My job is to handle her safety.

I watch Marie rub her cunt and moan, throwing her head back. I grin as Melina moves to kneel in front of her, across from my seat on the limo. Careful never to turn her head toward me, my friend goes to town on the bitch's pussy.

Cain's equally vigilant, so his face never appears on the video I'm filming from the camera hidden on the lapel of my jacket. He stands next to Marie's seat, the pants of his tux open at the crotch. She doesn't need to be told to take his cock in her mouth.

I don't move. I don't think I even see any of them. All that matters to me is that I have another pawn.

I don't know who tried to take Nadia off my board. I have too many enemies. Those who want me. Those who want to use me. And the many who just hate me.

There isn't a shadow of a doubt in my mind. That fire that burned her, scarred her skin was about me. And I'll repay that debt with interest, in charred flesh and spilled blood.

CHAPTER FOUR

Tall gilded gates, even higher tuition, and a small army of guards keep the rabble out of Cross and Roses, one of the most exclusive secondary schools in the country. Sitting in the back of my uncle's Maserati, right behind my cousin, I feel my stomach drop as we approach.

For two years I was ignored. Then I made Jace look in my direction, and suddenly everyone knew exactly who I was, for the worst reasons. Just like that, he set the entire school against me. By November, he and I were...whatever we were. Since the school dances to his tune, that meant that they started to leave me alone.

What now? I broke up with him. I just don't know what to expect. In a way, I preferred when I was sure I was walking into a lion's den last fall. The uncertainty is more daunting.

Lucius slows to a stop where the long line dropping

kids off after the Christmas break starts. Parents aren't allowed within the building unless they have appointments, so everyone is leaving their kids here.

He turns to me and smiles, though it doesn't reach his usually warm brown eyes.

My uncle's a handsome Italian man in his early forties. Several of my friends call him a DILTF, and snicker lewd comments I try to bleach out of my mind for my sanity. I've seen his kindness, his gentleness, his care. I've also seen his wrath. Since my accident, he's letting me glimpse something new. Coldness.

He's pissed about what happened to me. Not just pissed, freaked too. I've never seen him as scared as the Sunday night he burst into my hospital room, half an hour earlier than my own parents, demanding to know who was responsible and swearing to make them pay.

Come to think of it, he's not unlike a certain boy I've tried to banish from my mind.

In vain.

"You're sure you want to go back to this school? I can enroll you somewhere in the city."

I shake my head, though I'm not that certain it's wise. But what choice do I have? Switching school halfway through the year in my senior year? I might as well kiss my dream of attending Tisch goodbye. I'm not that good a student, and at a new school I'll take forever to catch up. "I'm fine, *Tio*, really. It was just a freak accident."

I don't believe that. He doesn't believe that. Even the super dumb princess from *Enchanted* wouldn't believe that. But saying it makes me feel better, and for all his worry, my uncle approves of my standing my ground. That's what he would do. We're Astrellas, after all.

He redirects his attention to his son. "You'll look after her."

That's not a question so much as an order, to which Lucas nods darkly.

I roll my eyes. Right. For all two or three days per month he'll turn up at school.

My cousin's finished most of his course requirements and could have graduated by now. He told me he still needs to pass PE, but I think that's bullshit; the only reason why he's coming to school at all is me. Checking on me, making sure I'm fine. This school full of privileged assholes can be a nightmare for those singled out, as I discovered last semester. Things might have been a lot worse for me, if Lucas hadn't occasionally checked in. He's sufficiently popular, and he made no secret of being in my corner, though I don't think many people realize we're related. On days he was around, I was left alone. Mostly.

I'm guessing that's why Uncle Lucius is dropping us off together this morning: to make a statement. Show the world that I'm not without protection.

Usually, Lucas would have driven his Audi and I would have come in the Hulk, my new, and highly problematic, Mini. Uncle Lucius insisted to get it looked at by the exceedingly expensive shop taking care of his cars, and then Lucas suggested his car might need a tune-up too.

Right. They're both protective idiots. No one is going to care who I come to school with. No one's going to notice.

"Keep your eyes open, kiddos. *Both* of you. You see anything amiss, don't hold your punches."

I hesitate before nodding. I'm not one to punch my way out of problems, and I've never really had to watch out for what's going on around me. I mean, last semester, I had to be more vigilant to avoid projectiles and wayward limbs thrown in my way to trip me over, but that's not what my uncle is cautioning me against now. There's someone seriously deranged, someone capable of harming a fellow human—and of beheading cats—after me.

Am I ready to walk back in this place?

I fake a bright smile and kiss his cheeks before exiting the vehicle, dragging my suitcase behind me.

Ready or not, I walk through the gates of Cross.

———

I drop my suitcase at the entrance of the common dorm, and immediately make my way to the bus taking us to the main building. Lucas hesitates, spotting a few of his friends waving at him.

"Go," I tell him, rolling my eyes.

He shakes his head. "I'll accompany you."

"You can't stick to me all day, every day. I'll be fine. It's seven thirty and the buses are packed." Nothing's going to happen to me in public. At worst, they'll throw insults at me, like they usually do, but to be frank, those roll off my back.

Lucas doesn't seem certain of himself, but he does end up listening to reason. "Text me if there's anything."

"Like you answer my texts."

He smirks and jogs over to his soccer buddies.

The moment he's gone, I lift my noise-cancelling headphones to my ears. Before I start the device, a girl I pass in front of grins at me. "Love the new hair, Nadia. Badass."

I'm too confused to reply. That's Jacqueline Billington, best friend of Yuki Moore. My last interaction with Yuki made it clear that she considers Jason hers, though that's only based on some bullshit agreement their parents made when they were kids, so we're not like to see eye to eye. Though to be fair, I'm not with Jason. Maybe she's cool with me now. And maybe I'll see a horde of unicorn run past.

That aside, those legacies have never given me the time of the day. They're too posh to lower themselves to the level of bullies, but they act like I'm a thorn in their four-inch stilettos. Their contempt sets the tone and shows the rest of the school who's fair game.

"Want a lift?" she offers, tilting her head toward the white town car with a uniformed driver waiting.

The trap is so obvious I snort. "Pass." I walk past her, toward the second bus.

The school grounds are too extensive to reach everything on foot, so they run throughout the day between the administrative building and dorms to the U-shaped eyesore where we have most of our classes.

"Hey, Nadia! Wanna sit with us?" I blink at the smiling girl I don't know.

She looks a little younger, maybe a junior or a sopho-more. She wears too much bright pink lip gloss and her high pony tails are adorable. I remember those who bullied me to my face, and she isn't one of them, but she also never bothered to speak to me until today.

I'm marginally more polite in my refusal as I head toward an empty seat at the back. "No, thank you."

Half of the bus talks to me on my way. They say hi. They enquire about my recovery. The moment I sit, the two boys in front of me turn to ask about my pain level.

What the fuck?

Being back at school feels strange, for an array of reasons, one of them being that in the month and a half since I left, my status was upgraded from pariah to person of relevance.

I trust it as much as I would trust a big bright box with Pandora's name on it.

"Hey, Nadia." I would swear the girl smiling at me bruised my ankle my second day at Cross and Roses. I shoot her the finger and everyone in the hallway chuckles at her expense.

She blushes and tucks her head down, hunching over as she rushes to her locker. That wasn't exactly kind, but really, what did she expect?

I hate almost everyone here. More importantly, I

don't trust them. Someone among them tried to *kill me*. And did kill Cat, my friend. She was called Bella, but using the silky feline's real name never fails to bring tears to my eyes, so I don't.

I really think whoever decapitated the poor pet is also responsible for setting fire to the dorms and locking my room, because really, can there be more than one person that crazy in one school? I refuse to believe I could have incensed two psychos. The incidents have to be related.

Maybe I'm too hopeful, but condensing the issue makes me feel better. It means I only have one enemy to unmask and destroy. I'll settle for unmasking, myself. Jason's better at destruction. I plan to just sit back and watch him work.

Whatever his intentions toward me, I don't doubt that he'll do what he promised to the one who attacked me. Wolves don't enjoy when another predator pisses on their territory. It's about his pride more than my safety.

I'm on my way to my calculus class when I hear my name being called out through the halls.

"Ms. Reyes, Ms. Nadia Reyes for the headmaster immediately, thank you."

Crap.

CHAPTER FIVE

I spent a fair bit of time in Ms. Casey's office in September, but I was always the one to call the meeting—I've never been summoned to the faculty building in my two and a half years as a student here. My grades might be average, but they've never been bad enough to warrant the attention of the instructors, and I'm not one to misbehave.

What the hell could they want with me now?

It has to be about the fire. They're either going to apologize for my getting hurt on school grounds, or update me on their investigation. I would have much preferred to go right back to class, but I can't exactly blow off the headmaster.

I head out of my calculus class, just in time to catch the bus waiting at the entrance of the U. I'm relieved to make it. There are over a dozen buses coming from the dorms and admin building first thing in the morning, but far less throughout the day. It's too cold for me to walk back this time of year, and besides, I'd arrive pretty late if I did.

The driver sings off-key to a French song I've heard a thousand times, "La vie en rose." It's one of my mother's favorites. I should find it comforting, but instead, I suddenly feel vulnerable. I'm alone with a stranger. Sure, he's an employee of this school, but no one said it was a kid who tried to kill me. Not to mention, my fellow students are all loaded. How much could it cost to bribe a driver to take a little detour by a shallow grave?

I'm getting seriously paranoid.

I listen to two verses before hooking my noise-cancelling headphones to my ears and playing something else until he drops me off in the courtyard between the dorms and the administrative building.

I don't often see the headmaster, Mr. Bone, outside of the ridiculous speeches he gives at the start of the year or whenever someone messes up badly enough for him to have to pretend to do some work. I'm sure a meeting was called after the fire, but I was hooked up to morphine in my hospital bed, safe from his tedious grandiloquence.

A tall, bald man with a mustache and long sleek hair, always in a striped suit, he seems rather intimidating from afar. When I'm ushered into his office, I see another person altogether. There's sauce at the corner of his mouth—dried mustard, I think—and he stinks of tobacco. Some things are much shinier from a distance.

"Ms. Reyes." He's standing behind an oak desk, and

his beady blue eyes narrow on me as he leans forward, hands flat on either side of a computer. "Quite the trouble you've caused."

I'm downright confused. Trouble, me? I haven't even been here since the week before Thanksgiving, and before then, I'd certainly not caused any trouble. If anything, this school was happy to keep their eyes closed when shit was happening *to me,* but I've never done anything reprehensible.

"We've investigated the fire. What happened was no accident, was it?" The headmaster smirks at me knowingly.

That seems obvious, but he doesn't seem like someone concerned about one of his students being targeted. He looks like a cat staring at a mouse. What is he suggesting?

"We take these matters extremely seriously, Ms. Reyes. Smoking is forbidden in any part of our establishment, let alone in the dorms."

What the fuck? "I don't smoke."

"The investigation was clear: the fire was the result of a cigarette. You smoked with the door closed, caused extensive damage to a hundred-year-old building, and endangered the lives of countless students. I should expel you for that."

I swallow hard. Expel me? Shit. Changing schools in January would have been bad enough for my transcript, but an expulsion will destroy my future, my dreams of attending Tisch—or any decent college for that matter. I struggle to come up with a defense. I've never smoked a day in my life, but how can I prove it?

What am I even doing in his office if he planned on expelling me? I mean, it could have taken a few weeks for the investigation to determine the origin of the fire, but I suspect there's something else at play.

He said he *should* expel me, not that he would.

It hits me then. This is another bullying technique. The faculty has been in on Jason's game from the start. Mr. Bone intends to push things further by unjustly punishing me for a crime I didn't commit. I bet it wasn't a cigarette at all, or if it was, it certainly didn't come from my room. He just wants an excuse to lash out, in order to please a twisted kid who doesn't know what he wants.

Really, Jason?

I knew he wasn't going to take the breakup well, but this is low, even for him.

My mouth flattens into straight line and I keep silent. I opt to see how this plays out before deciding. As I wait, I realize the likelihood of my having to transfer schools is much higher than it was this morning. I'm sure Uncle Lucius won't mind arranging it if I asked.

"Look, I don't smoke. If you found a cigarette butt, get it tested for my DNA, fingerprints, or whatever the police do to determine the culprit. It won't be me."

"I should, in fact, get the authorities involved," he agrees. "You're fortunate the school board frowns at drawing such attention. Don't push your luck, young lady. The fire came from your room. If you keep denying your involvement, I won't have any choice but to call the police, and when they prove that it was you, the consequences will be much more severe than if you'd come clean today."

Fuck. I'm eighteen. The last thing I need is a record as a pyro. I know I didn't do anything, but what if they can't —or won't—prove it? Shit. Do I need a lawyer?

"The only reason why you boast the privilege of staying here, and out of prison, is because your uncle has supported Cross and Roses for years. We value his contribution, and we value your cousin's grades." Not mine, needless to say.

Lucas's test scores are crazy high, and ensure Cross remains one of the top private schools in the country. I'm average at best.

"But regardless of your connections, your offense will *not* be left unpunished." He grins, relishing every second of this farce, like the dick on a power trip he is. "You will make up your debt to the school with community service, aiding the janitors every day after class, until the end of the year."

He can't be fucking serious. Lucius pays almost fifty thousand per year so I can study at Cross—an entire salary for median households in some states—and he wants me to provide free labor on top of that? I don't balk at getting my hands dirty, and I'm no stranger to cleaning, having helped out at my father's restaurant many times since I was a teenager, but this is something else. He *knows* what that would do to me, how it will change the way my peers treat me in this school. The kids enrolled here are ruthless to anyone who isn't wealthy and powerful.

I'm half Latina, half Italian, and my parents don't have millions; that was enough for people to pretend I didn't exist for years. Put a broomstick in my hands and that's an invitation to give me shit for life. I don't think the bulk of the student corp is racist—they don't mind *rich* brown kids—but they're completely elitist. Things might have been bad for me in the fall, but this edict would make my life literal *hell*.

I'm just about to tell him where he can shove his community service when the door opens behind me.

With all the confidence in the world, like the entire place belongs to him—and it might as well—Jason strolls into the room, though he wasn't invited in. He doesn't even bother with an "excuse me."

The headmaster's face falls, looking both confused and subservient now. His smirk gives way to a professional mask. "Mr. Alden."

CHAPTER SIX

I don't like how my body immediately relaxes, all the
anxiety leaving me, which is freaking stupid. Why,
oh, why do I feel safe with Jason Alden?

My instincts are all wrong when it comes to him. He's
an asshole and my body should remember that.

I'm in this boat in the first place *because* of him. He's
the one who had both the student body and the administrative employees shit on me last term. Before this precise
moment, I actually thought he'd asked Mr. Bone to serve
this punishment. The old guy's expression invalidates that
theory: he looks like a child caught with his hands in the
cookie jar.

"John." Jason drags the metallic chair next to mine—
the one parents usually occupy—along the hardwood
floor and sits.

His hand moves to my thigh and squeezes it. I don't

know whether he means to comfort or intimidate me, but he manages both. "Where were we?"

That boy. Eighteen, and already the self-assurance of a king. I don't doubt he'll become a force to be reckoned with like his father.

Mr. Bone clears his throat. I shouldn't enjoy his visible discomfort at this reversal of our situations, but he certainly liked seeing me squirm. After his bullshit, I'm all for Jason giving him a little taste of his own medicine.

The headmaster's racking his brain, and before he comes up with some well-crafted lie wrapped up in a big bow, I opt to answer for him. "He was telling me that he'd like me to clean toilets or whatever for the rest of the year. See, he believes I cause the fire by smoking in my room—though he can't have proof, because I *didn't*." I smirk at Mr. Bone. "I was just about to let him know that I'll contact my uncle about switching to another school."

I hold my head high, delighted to be hitting two birds at once with that declaration. I'm telling that asshole of a teacher to fuck off, and showing Jason just how limited his power over me is.

Oh, he's one of the kings of Cross, it's true, but I *can* leave. If things get too bad for me, I will. It's not smart for my future, but the pro and con columns between leaving and staying are fairly even at my current status quo. If anyone pushes me too hard, I'm out of here.

I won't claim to understand Jason Alden, but I suspect he doesn't want me out of his grasp. He's not done with me. He wouldn't be sitting next to me otherwise.

His fingers tighten over my legs, digging into my skin. I shouldn't savor his lapse of control as much as I do, but here we are. I never said I was nice.

He shoots me that cold look I know all too well, silently communicating something along the lines of "I'll deal with you later." Then his steely eyes make the man shake in his striped suit. "Let me get things straight. One of your students is locked in her bedroom, while someone starts a fire in the utility closet across the hall, and you want to *punish* her?"

The headmaster's face is ashen, his eyes wide, like prey caught in a trap. He's also visibly confused. I don't doubt that's because just a few months ago, Jason was right in this same chair telling him to make things as difficult as possible for me.

I snatch his wrist and pry his hand off my leg, my eyes narrowing. God, he's such a dick.

"I thought you said the fire started in *my* room." I play dumb, batting my lashes innocently. "Which I found confusing as hell, as I was taking a shower—and I've never smoked in my entire life."

Mr. Bone sits, sweat dotting his forehead. "I was told the cigarette butt was found on the floor close to your room. It's only logical..."

In a rare show of kindness, Jace doesn't let him continue to embarrass himself with his flimsy excuse. "My father, who sits on the school board, ordered a thorough examination of the incident, John. The fire started in the utility closet—the cigarette butt was surrounded by flammable substances, and doused in gasoline, which makes it clear that the perpetrator had ill intent. You ought to have received the details by email." Jason's laidback countenance is hilarious, in contrast to *John's* increasing uneasiness. He seems bored with the entire conversation.

Mr. Bone stutters, "W—well, in that case..."

"How about you start with an apology?" Jason suggests. "Nadia has been relentlessly bullied since the beginning of the school year by multiple students, and the administration's indifference is unacceptable. My father *will* hear of this."

Oh, this is rich, coming from him, the source of literally all my problems. I'm stunned he can say that with a straight face.

The teacher is quick to blurt, "I *am* sorry for the confusion, Mr. Alden. Of course..."

"To her," Jason clarifies, throwing his arm across my chair.

I'm going to hell for enjoying Jason torturing the headmaster as much as I am, but I'm relishing the ride down to my doom.

"Certainly." Mr. Bone clears his throat, and forces his gaze to me. "My apologies, Ms. Reyes. I was operating under erroneous assumptions."

By that, he means that he thought Jason still wanted to fuck me over. I would swat his arm away from me, if his protection weren't the reason why this meeting did a one-eighty.

He's reestablished the status quo. Staying at Cross and Roses is still my best option again. For now.

"There will be no need for detention," the principal sputters, changing his tune completely.

"Investigating how the attack occurred might be an appropriate action, don't you think?"

Mr. Bone thinks whatever Jason tells him to think. "Of course, of course." He bobs his head up and down repetitively. If I opened his heart, I'd find a clockwork mechanism and strings tied to Jason's fingertips. "We take the safety of our students quite seriously."

So long as the legacies demand it, at least.

This place is seriously messed up.

"Glad to hear it." Jason stands, and I get to my feet too. "With that in mind, you'll arrange Nadia's move to my building by the end of the day."

I stare at him openmouthed. He can't mean that. I've never so much as stepped inside the modern glass mansion in front of the lake, and now he wants me to live there?

I don't even know who's more dangerous; him, his friends, his wannabe-wife, Yuki, or the psycho who tried to set me on fire.

"Wait a second..." I start to say.

Jason's hand, still around the back of my chair, moves to my neck. He digs his fingers into my tight muscles with a purpose.

I don't let his attempt at controlling me deter me. "I

can't move into Glass. Everyone in that building hates me."

"Dramatic, much?" He rolls his eyes. "You know the guys love you." By the guys, he must mean his friends, and I know no such thing. At best, they think me entertaining and like to rile me up. "I'm quite fond of you myself."

I don't bother to state the obvious: whoever wants to hurt me is probably in that building. It must be someone powerful, to have had access to my door keys and somehow made it inside the dorm and out without any guard or cameras catching them. "I'm not a legacy."

"I am." Jace is smooth as ever. "And you're mine."

It's the worst idea I've ever heard, and I'm certain it will incense whoever's after me.

"I don't want..."

"Your safety is more important than your desires, Nadia. Every inch of that building is recorded, no one can enter your room without a specific key card with a unique access code, and we have a security detail superior to the rest of Cross and Roses."

My jaw's still tight, but he makes a decent case. I guess I could try.

Except... "I'm not moving in with you."

"Of course not." He smirks, suspecting what I know: he's already won. My safety *is* more important than whatever other concerns I might have, and I'm not certain I'd feel safe back in the dorms after what happened in November. "You'll be across the hall."

The headmaster is just as flabbergasted as I am. "The

board will not approve. The school bylaws are rather strict; the lake house is reserved to a number of students considered at risk because of their family's standing—including Ms. Reyes would defeat its purpose." That's the closest thing to a protest that's crossed his lips since Jason entered the room.

Jason whips out his phone, his thumb flying over the screen until he places a call on speaker. The person on the other end replies after four rings, his voice low and authoritative. "Jace."

"Father. I do apologize for disturbing you during your work day. Mr. Bone is being problematic."

Now I almost feel bad for the poor headmaster. He looks about to piss his pants.

"You want me to have him replaced?" Mr. Alden offers without asking for details.

Jesus, these people are something else. I can't even imagine having that much power. No wonder Jason believes himself untouchable.

"Not for the moment. Can we just clarify what the board's position would be on moving my girlfriend to Glass?"

"The Astrella girl?"

I gape, openly shocked. Jason's father knows of me?

"Reyes," he corrects. "The school hasn't bothered to find who set the fire yet, so she could be in danger. I'd rather have her near me."

His father hesitates only one moment. "Remind Mr. Bone his jurisdiction doesn't extend to Glass—and won't extend to *any* Heritage-affiliated businesses if he doesn't remember his place. And take care of her. We don't need her father displeased with us."

"Uncle," Jason says. "And thank you. Say hi to Mother."

"You call her if you'd like to say anything. I'm in a meeting." Mr. Alden sounds gruff, but he did answer in the middle of a meeting. Father and son appear to share the strange ability of seeming both cold and caring. "Anything else?"

"No, I'll let you get back to work. Thanks for the clarification." Jace hangs up and tucks his phone back into his pocket with a tilt of his head to the headmaster. "Did you catch everything, or do I need to disrupt other board members?"

The poor guy's Adam's apple bobbles meekly. "I'll arrange the transfer, sir."

Sir. It's all I can do not to laugh.

"You do that." Jason wraps his arm around my waist, pulls me close and kisses the side of my head.

I let him make his point. It's only for show.

The moment we're out of the office, though, I wiggle out of his embrace and remind him of something we both need to keep in mind after this performance. "I'm not your girlfriend, Jace."

CHAPTER SEVEN

Jason shoves his hands in his pockets and walks out of the faculty building.

As soon as the automated doors leading to the courtyard open, a crisp coldness hits my nose, and I inch forward, grinning.

The first snowfall of the season. It was too warm earlier, so I doubt it'll stick, but I'm delighted all the same.

"You like winter," Jason guesses, watching my childish display of enthusiasm.

I grimace in distaste. Even in my red duffle coat, with thick socks under my Docs and fleece-lined tights, I'm freezing. "I'm a summer girl through and through, but there's something about snow."

I enjoy watching it fall, and waking up to a white morning the first time it sticks is a vision out of a fairy tale or a dream. It never fails to make me smile.

"Have you seen it from high up in the mountains? The Alps, or Aspen?" He asks, guiding us toward his driver, who waits in front of the burgundy Bentley.

As far as cars go, it's one of the most modest ones among those who keep a driver just to take them from their dorms to the school. If I've learned one thing at Cross, is that those with true wealth don't tend to flaunt it too hard.

I could wait for a bus, but his car is already here, and I see no harm in getting in. It means nothing, other than the fact that I prefer convenience. Besides, I just agreed to move into Glass—getting a ride from him is nothing in comparison.

"Right. The Alps. I go every other day." What kind of person does he think I am?

Jason chuckles, and holds his hand up to the driver, who's just walked out of the front of the car. The man— young, attractive, and dark haired—nods and return to his seat.

Jason opens the back door for me, and I slide into the large passenger area, set up like a limo's.

Inside, the car's delightfully warm. I relax on the black butter-soft leather seat.

"I figured your uncle might have taken you on a skiing holiday." Jason sits next to me, closes the door, and the car starts immediately.

A credible assumption, but an erroneous one all the same. "I've never skied. It's not really Uncle Lucius's thing, and even if it was, he rarely has time for a long vacation."

"I'll take you." The offer crosses his lips easily.

I snort. I guess that brings us right back to my previous point. "I already told you: I'm not your girl-friend, Jason. You're not taking me anywhere." Except back to class, but that's not the point.

"Do we have to do this now?" His car has almost reached the U, and he vaguely waves toward it. "We have class."

"We don't have to do anything. I'm just telling it like it is. At no point have I ever been your girlfriend, and given that I've told you I'd like to stop hanging out, I'm even less so now." My voice rises and speeds up. "Why would I go with you to France, or even Colorado, for Christ's sake!"

I'm not even certain why I sound so upset. I'm not, I'm just stating a fact I need him to acknowledge, going forward.

At Jason's long-suffering sigh, I open my mouth to keep pushing my point.

I don't get to.

Before another word crosses my lips, one of his hands is around my neck and the other, sliding along my thighs and then cupping my pussy. Somehow, even through the thick layers of clothing, his hands burn me. Heat immedi-ately ignites at my core, and I can't think of anything past his touch.

"We've arrived, sir," I hear through speakers probably connected to the driver at the front.

The car has already stopped by the main gate. I didn't even notice. Not when the hand against my core moves underneath my clothing and slips against my folds.

"I'm aware, David." I can feel Jason's smooth chuckle, close as he is. "We're not ready yet. You might prefer to close the partition."

Then his mouth is on mine, and I lose sense of space and time. God, I missed the harsh softness of his lips, and the way my body responds to him. I know I have to keep telling him that we're not together until it sticks, until he gets that I don't intend to resume our sick version of a relationship, but none of that seems relevant or important while he's kissing me.

I want more. I need more. And I take it.

A moan on my lips, I open to taste the tip of his tongue and lap at it. Jason grins as he meets me stroke for stroke. His hand around my neck tightens and guides me lower, till my back hits the seats. Hovering over me, Jason moves both hands to my hips. He grasps all the layers of clothing and slides them along my legs in one go.

I glance toward the front of the car, and notice the driver looking into his rearview mirror.

Oh my god!

"He can see," I whisper.

Jason smirks knowingly, and I remember his words. *You might prefer to close the partition.* He didn't *tell* his employee to do so, and apparently, David prefers to watch us.

"Jason…"

"Tell me in a moment." Without further preamble, he bends over me and puts his mouth right at my pussy, rendering me insane with the first lick.

Jason eats me out like he has all the time in the world, exploring every single one of my folds again and again, as his hands dig into my hips. Mine curl around his soft hair, keeping him right there. The damn butterflies rage in my stomach as my insides burn.

"Jace, I—"

His middle finger joins his mouth, curving inside me.

Back arching, I glance at the driver again. He's still staring. I can't decide how that makes me feel. Having sex with Jason at his club was one thing, but we're right at the front of our school, and this man's his employee. David looks a little like Captain America, if Chris Evans wore rectangular glasses and had longer hair. He's older than us —somewhere close to thirty, at least. He has a bit of stubble on his strong jaw and a muscular body under his dark suit. He looks like he's on his way to court or the financial district. Are we *really* doing this in front of him?

I could tell him to look away. I *should*.

I watch him smile at me in the mirror and my core tightens.

Another one of Jason's fingers slides inside me, and starts to move in and out. "Fuck. Fuck, Jace."

"Soon, doll. I'll be inside you soon, I promise you that.

For now, just come on my fingers while David wanks himself looking at your gorgeous cunt."

Oh god, he isn't...I glance at the driver again, and notice that his right arm seems to be moving. Jesus. "Do you like watching Nadia, David?"

"Very much so, sir."

"That's all right. She enjoys it. Don't you, pretty doll?"

My nipples tighten under my clothes. I feel his touch *everywhere*, so sensitive I could cry.

I'm embarrassed and ashamed of feeling this way, but I don't think my body's ever been this tight, this out of control. I *do* enjoy watching some hot, older stranger looking at me like this. It should be wrong. It *is* wrong. I simply don't care.

I almost explode, so fucking sensitive the merest flick drives me wild. I'm sure they can hear me scream all the way in my calculus class.

Jason's gaze seeks mine as he directs his mouth to my clit, sucking it.

"Jace," I beg.

His hand pumps faster and faster, while his tongue laps slowly, maddeningly, bringing me closer to the precipice, until I don't have a choice. I fall.

I think I lose it for a moment. When my head clears up, Jason's back on his seat, licking his fingers clean.

His tongue runs over his lower lip, then he throws his schoolbag over his shoulder.

"Shouldn't you get ready? I mean, if you'd like to go to

school like that, I don't mind. I can just bend you over and take you as the need arises."

I'm so fucking flustered. My entire face is on fire as I crumple my clothing to my chest and rush to pull my tights on, then my skirt.

I consciously force myself not to look at the driver. David. I suppose I should refer to him with his first name, if only in my head. He's seen me getting licked out until I yelled. He's wanked to it. It kinda feels like we should be on first-name basis after all that.

Once I'm dressed, Jason opens the door.

He doesn't even bother to say anything, confident he's made his point because I can't resist his touch.

He doesn't know me at all.

As we cross the entryway, I tap his shoulder to get his attention, get to my tiptoes and kiss the side of his face. "Thanks for the orgasm. You're still not my boyfriend, Jason. Just my sex toy."

I wink, and walk toward my Italian class. Calculus is almost over anyway.

CHAPTER EIGHT

After a casual round of semipublic sex, my morning is utterly ordinary.

I see Sophia in Italian, and she asks me how I'm doing before class starts. The fact that she needs the update says a lot about our decaying friendship. We've texted a couple of times over the last weeks, but that's about it.

My answer's a fake smile and an even more false "fine! You look great, by the way," and thankfully, Signora Di Maio walks in, cutting the conversation short.

My energy's all over the place when I'm on my way to AP English, one of the classes I share with Jason. We have that, our lunch period, and history in common. Well, and our PE class, but like the rest of the jocks, he does endurance training with Ms. Palmer, while we plebians suffer under the guidance of Mr. Pierson, so we're rarely even in the same room. But in English and history, I can't avoid him even if I try.

I'm one of the first to arrive, before Mr. Green walks in.

Melina, already seated, squeals when she sees me. "Damn, girl! That hair is *fire*."

It's not the first compliment I've heard today, but at least this time I know it's sincere. Even when the entire school was bullying me, Melina was kind, so I actually trust her more than most.

"Thanks." I slide into the seat to her left. "You had a good holiday break?"

She snorts. "Yeah, right. Five Fullers in the same house for two weeks? It's a miracle we all made it out alive. How 'bout you, you get along with your folks?"

I nod enthusiastically. "Dad's busy, but he's nice, you know. And he's basically is very hands-off, parenting wise. My mother was pretty strict when I was growing up, but she's been chill the last few years." Manuela Reyes was never overly controlling, but she had a thing about wanting to know where I was all the time. I'd go out with my friends after school to skate or get some ice cream, and she'd lose it if I arrived an hour late. I've never quite understood her fear, so I wasn't that great at texting her with updates.

That might be why Uncle Lucius decided to send me to boarding school, come to think of it. And it worked. My mother and I get along just fine now.

"No one really gives a shit about what I do, so long as

I have okay grades and stay out of *Page Six*. That must be nice, to have a parent who cares."

I frown at Melina. "Yours don't?"

"My mom's always busy helping some charity and my dad works all the time. You know, the typical story." She shrugs. "I can't complain."

Cain walks in just as the last bell rings just as, grinning at me. "Damn, cupcake." He aims straight for me and sits at the desk right in front of me. "You look good enough to eat. 'Sup, Mel." He winks at her, charming as ever.

"You'd know if you answered your texts. I need you to get back to me about the plane. Are we traveling in yours this year?"

He frowns. "Why do we always take mine?"

"Because the parents travel in the Eatons', and my folks tell the staff not to serve us alcohol. Come on, *please*?"

For a hot second, I almost had the impression I was chatting with two normal kids. The whole private plane topic certainly put things in perspective.

"How about asking Jason for a change? Alden Corps' jet is lit."

"It's a company plane; Jason has to jump through hoops to use it. You know he won't bother." Melina makes good use of her sensual, pouty lips and bats her long lashes. "Please?"

Cain lets her win. "Fine. You owe me a blowjob."

Melina grins smugly, clearly happy with that compromise.

"Going somewhere nice?" I ask just to be polite, and because Mr. Green isn't here yet.

Nor is Jason. And I don't care. Hell, I don't even notice. And I certainly do not steal a glance at the door every now and then.

"London. The Heritage meets up every January to talk about our stats."

"Stats?" I echo.

"How much we gave to charity, the number of aspiring members we're vetoing, that kind of thing. It's just an excuse to get wasted and brag about stuff."

"Why London? I thought the Heritage was an American club."

Like the greater part of the population, I didn't know many details about the club, really, other than the fact that it's super-exclusive and secretive. They give millions to charity every year and throw socialite parties that never fail to bring paparazzi to their door, given the fact that half of their members are celebrities.

Thanks to Jason, I'm now also aware of the fact that most members are into deviant stuff. Swinging, kinky sex, I don't exactly know.

Watching. I think back to the Captain America looka-like jerking off as Jace finger- and tongue-fucked me, and I flush all over.

Definitely watching.

"Technically," Mel replies. "But the Heritage was built by members of a secret society in London, so the two clubs are sort of cousins."

"More like rivals," Cain snorts.

Mel nods in agreement. "One year, the annual review's in New York, the next, in London."

I shake my head. "Your life is out of a cheesy movie."

Mr. Green walks in, dragging a large TV on a wheeled shelf, just as the two legacies chuckle at my comment. "I apologize for the delay, but I have a surprise for you! I figured it'd be nice to ease back to work. Today's TV Day. If you wouldn't mind drawing the blinds..."

Mel leans toward me. "I bet you fifty bucks he's hungover."

"Not taking that fool's bet."

After the TV's set up, we watch the first episode of the BBC version of *Wuthering Heights*. I haven't seen it before, but I still freaking hate every single character in that story.

Jason doesn't make an appearance at any point in the next hour and a half. When the bell rings, I close my notebook and stuff it in my bag.

Cain turns to face me. "You can ask, you know."

I guess exactly what he means, as there's only one burning question in my mind, but I decide to feign ignorance. "Ask what?" I'm *dying* to know where Jason is, but I'll be damned if I let anyone know that.

Because if Cain knows, Jason will know.

The dark-haired asshole scoffs. "What the lady doesn't ask, she doesn't get. You're eating with us?"

My refusal is instant. "I don't think so."

I might not entirely dislike Cain, though I trust him

about as far as I could throw him, but lunch with a tableful of legacies isn't my idea of fun.

"Suit yourself, but we'll save you a place." He reaches out for my arm and pretends to hit it in slow motion, barely touching me. "You're one of us, now."

The strange thing is, the way they spoke to me today? It almost feels like I am.

I don't know what to make of any of this, but I don't trust it.

CHAPTER NINE

I eat at my usual table, glad for a sense of drama-free normality for a while. Besides, it's nice catching up with my surface lunch time friends.

The one notable absence from our usual party is Sophia. A sweeping glance around the cafeteria shows me she's seated at the popular table, next to Yuki, and only three seats away from her sister.

I noticed in Italian, and I'm struck by her appearance again. Sophia's almost unrecognizable. She's lost tons of weight in the last few months, and her natural makeup makes her skin appear perfect and glowing. Part of me is happy for her. Proud, even. She came out of her shell after the It Girls embraced her. She also dumped me like an old shoe, but I don't mind, so whatever. Good for her.

When I look at Brooke, I catch her shooting daggers at Sophia and smile to myself. Serves her right. Brooke bullied her little sister relentlessly for years. Seeing Sophia get along so well with the true queen bee of the school has *got* to sting.

I sit next to Willow, indifferent to Sophia's absence by now. As usual, the redhead piled her plate up with a ton of food, and I have no clue where she packs it.

Alexander tells us about his chess competition in Russia. He beat a player ranked second worldwide and earned a fat lump of cash in the process.

"I bet twenty bucks on you," Willow says, surprising everyone around the table.

I hadn't known Alexander had a competition, but if I had, I wouldn't have gone to the trouble of checking on him, let alone placing a bet. We're not that kind of friends. Maybe Willow, abrasive as she might seem, cares more than the rest of us. Or maybe she fancies Alex.

I can't see it, though. Not only because he's average and Willow's objectively a bombshell, but because she seems entirely oblivious to the other sex. Not even Jason ruffles her feathers. Maybe she's asexual.

"How did you do it?" Elisa asks. "Don't you have to be over twenty-one to gamble?"

"Online. My sister's twenty-three, and we share a common account for bills and stuff. I just put in her details. It made me over five hundred bucks. I wish I could have spared more than a twenty, the odds were insane."

The reminder that twenty bucks is the maximum that she could have spared is somewhat comforting. It reassures me that there are some normal people around me. I think back to the whole private plane conversation with the legacies, and smile. Willow is my kind of person.

"Congrats on your win, too, I guess." Alexander grins at her. "And thanks for the vote of confidence."

I'm almost done with my meal when I feel a prickle at the back of my neck, and automatically glance over my shoulder. Jason strolls in, his arm around the shoulder of none other than Marie Vaughn.

Marie fucking Vaughn.

As in, the asshole who destroyed my sculpture of Stheno in art class.

Blasé as ever, he strolls to the table he shares with Cain, Maverick, and Rowan, and takes a seat, while Marie fetches his food tray and hers.

All of a sudden, I feel sick to my stomach. I could hit something. I *want* to punch something so bad. Just hours ago, he had his face between my legs and was calling me his, and now he's parading that *bitch* around?

Jason stares right at me and has the nerve to smile.

Smile.

My fists tighten around my knife and fork.

"Nadia!" Willow's frowning at me when I turn to her. I don't think it's the first time she's called my name.

"Sorry, woolgathering. You were saying?"

"Are you going to Italy, Germany, or France?"

I'm confused, before I remember about the cultural travel abroad happening in three months. "Oh yeah, the spring trip, right? None of them." I shrug. "I can't afford it."

I never join the school's ridiculously expensive excursions. My first year at Cross, they planned a week in Los Angeles for eleven thousand bucks per person. *Eleven.*

Last year, it was Australia. This year, the seniors are leaving with the language teacher and the cost of the trip is twenty freaking thousand dollars.

I'm sure Uncle Lucius would pay for it if I asked, but he's already so generous, I'd hate to take advantage. Therefore, I didn't even mention it.

Willow winces. "Yeah, I couldn't exactly swing that kind of money either. My scholarship is paying for it."

Elisa whistles. "That's one hell of a scholarship, then. I don't think Sarah Jones or Jeremy Sutton are coming."

Sarah's in my gym class—she's here on an athletic scholarship. I don't know Jeremy, but I've heard the name thrown around—he's the president of the journalism club, among several other equally nerdy occupations.

"My sister's married to a legacy," Willow tells us.

My jaw falls. It's the first I've heard about that. Just moments ago, I thought she was a normal person, like me.

Willow's a hard worker, always paying attention to money and I was under the impression she was struggling.

And she could still be, I guess. Just because one of her family members married into money doesn't mean that she's rich.

"Seriously?"

"Not one from the East Coast. He's part of the Californian Heritage. He got me into Cross. I mean, the school decided to grant me the scholarship, but he's the one who made them look at my file in the first place. I'm guessing that's why my package includes an overpriced trip to Paris." She grimaces. "Or maybe he's just paying for it, I don't know. I don't *want* to know, really, because otherwise I'll have to decline his help...and I really want fresh croissants."

"Damn," Elisa says. "So, you're a mini-legacy."

She laughs like she's never heard a funnier joke. "Yeah, right. My parents are both in jail and I lived in a trailer until I was fourteen. Absolute legacy material."

I'm fascinated. "How did your sister meet her husband?

"In my hometown, there was a private and a public school. You can guess where we used to go. But one of our friends transferred in her senior year, and started dating a rich guy. They got married right out of high school." She rolls her eyes. "Anyway, my sister and Camden were maid of honor and best man at the wedding three years ago. I wasn't there while they dated—my mother got arrested and I ended up in a foster home around the same time."

She drones on about what she knows of her sibling's misadventure, and I'm grateful for the distraction, though I still feel Jason's stare searing into my back.

Despite attempting to focus on Willow, part of my mind stays on Jason and his fucking audacity. I know exactly what he's doing: trying to piss me off, to prove to me that I care.

Shoulders tight, I hang on Willow's every word. I

think I say the right things at the right moments. Her sister's relationship seems at least as dramatic as mine, and any other day, I wouldn't have to fake my interest. Today, it's struggle to stay focused, but I manage.

I follow the group out when we're done eating, and walk to PE with Willow, forcing myself not to spare any thought for Jason fucking Alden.

That, I mostly fail at.

CHAPTER TEN

P E's not as bad as it could be. I mean, I abhor every second of it, as they force us to play badminton indoors, and I have the coordination of a demented ostrich when it comes to sports involving a racket. At least no one trips me up, and the teacher doesn't seem intent on singling me out, which is a lovely change.

I drag my feet in the showers, reluctant to get to history, but I eventually have to get moving.

I arrive with the last bell, and as usual, my gaze immediately converges on Jason. I force my eyes away and plaster a pleasant smile as I wave back at Rowan like I have no care in the world. Like I don't see Jason's arm around the shoulders of the bitch who destroyed my art.

There's an open seat one row in front of Jason, smack in the middle of the class, but I ignore it, favoring one in the front row.

I don't hear a word Mr. Michaels says, but I fake being fascinated and attentive well enough for him to not ask me to participate.

When the class ends, my instincts want me to rush out, but I'm an Astrella, and my pride sings a different song. I take my time to pack up.

As I expected, Jason's steps soon approach. "Your room's ready." He leans back against the closest desk and has the audacity to smile at me. "You're going to love Glass."

"What could possibly make you believe you know anything about what I love, Alden?"

"You're not wrong." Jace smirks. "I only know you love art, and parties with your friends in the city, and, let's not forget, the way my mouth feels against your pussy. I'm looking forward to learning more about you, doll."

"Suck a dick. How many times do I have to tell you I'm not interested in whatever you're offering?"

"Just like you weren't interested in the car. Just like you won't be interested when you're taking my cock deep in your mouth later."

I don't miss the way his eyes zero in on my lips.

I shiver, but I hide it. Outwardly, I treat him exactly like what he is: some random guy in my class. "Whatever you say, Jace. Catch you later." I leave the room and don't look back.

To my relief, he lets me.

Every moment with him is humiliating, exhausting,

and the more time I spend with him, the more I lose who I am—who I was before him.

I can't get attached to him.

I won't.

———————

I just have art class before the end of my school day. It's only been six weeks since the burns, and my skin's still painful and tight in places, so I don't want to go to swim club yet.

I head out of the school with the throng of students and start to queue in front of the bus as usual, when it hits me: the buses don't even go to Glass.

Almost all of the legacies have drivers, and those who don't carpool.

Reaching the lake should only take about twenty minutes on foot, but it's freezing out here. I guess I could take the bus to the dorms and walk from there, cut the walk down to maybe ten minutes.

Letting Jason move me to his building seems like a worse and worse idea every minute, and I haven't even seen the place yet. I'm weighing my options when a sleek, black sedan stops in front of me.

The back window rolls down and Melina tilts her head. "Hop in!"

I don't hesitate, gratefully opening the door and stepping into the warmth of the luxurious interior. Before I close the door, I notice the company and I freeze.

Like Jace's car, this one has a large passenger area with two rows of seats facing each other. Mel sits facing the driver's back, and directly opposite her sit Yuki Moore and Manon Montgomery.

Manon is a ridiculously perfect, smooth-skinned, doe-eyed, black Barbie. Tall and limber, she's a cheerleader. I don't have anything against her per se, other than the company she keeps. I even remember her coming to my defense that one time, though her effort was lackluster.

"Can you close the door?" Manon crosses her endless legs. "It's freezing."

I obey, though I feel like I've been trapped in a spiderweb.

I do as I'm told, and the car starts again. We remain in complete silence for all of three seconds, then Manon starts chatting, presumably resuming the conversation going on before my arrival. "So, Monique's with Laura, you know."

I *don't* know, but I don't interrupt.

"And Laura's been into Benjamin Lawrence forever. Monique asked Benny boy if he'd like a threesome with both of them for Laura's birthday. Except Benjamin basically only fucked Monique, and now Laura's pissed at basically both of them. She's trying to fuck Rowan, because she knows he's Monique's wet dream."

I don't have a clue who Laura, Monique, or Benjamin Lawrence are, but the way Manon talks about sex, so perfunctorily, reminds me what company I'm in.

I'm certain Willow, Elisa, and Alexander don't chat

about threesomes like it's a walk on the beach on a sunny Sunday afternoon.

"Rowan, as in Rowan White?" Melina laughs. "Good luck to her. He'll *never* go for a freshman."

I'd be a hypocrite by turning my nose up at the notion of unusual sexual preferences, but imagining freshmen in a threesome is somewhat disturbing to me. I hadn't even kissed a guy at that age. When I look at freshmen these days, they're basically babies to me.

None of the women in the car seem to share my opinion.

"A little makeup, a push-up bra, and she could manage it, if he's drunk enough." Yuki smirks. "I've done worse at fifteen."

I grimace in distaste but don't comment one way or another. "Thanks for the lift," I say, to be polite.

I'm looking at Melina, but Yuki replies, "You're welcome."

Shit, this is her car?

"After all, I hear we're neighbors now." She might be smiling, but her cool glare gives me the creeps. "How did that happen, by the way?"

Three pairs of eyes focus on me. They want an explanation, and I don't have one at the ready. I'm certainly not about to mention Jason in front of Yuki. He's the one who arranged for me to move to Glass, but if I say so, so many questions would follow to which I don't have satisfactory answers.

"It's because of the fire. They're renovating, and I think they didn't have a room for me in the main dorm."

Thankfully, the car's stopped in front of the humongous modern lake house, so I open the door and exit the vehicle before they question my stupid-ass lie.

CHAPTER ELEVEN

I'm the first to exit the car in front of the lake house. Steps away from the entrance, I hesitate, not even sure *how* I'm supposed to walk in. Maybe I should have stopped by the faculty building first, so that someone could show me inside.

The three legacies bypass me and advance toward the double doors.

The lake house, as its sobriquet suggests, is a designer mansion entirely made of reflective glass in different shades, except for the upper floor. It's impossible to see that high up from the ground, but I think the fifth floor looks like it's made of regular glass, where the inside might be visible from out here.

This building, shaped like irregular waves, is the one place most of the students have never seen the inside of on the school campus. Myself included.

There are bonfires at the lakeside some weekends, and

the legacies often throw after-parties in Glass. They invite *some* students from the regular dorms, but I never made the cut. Their selection extended to popular people like Brooke or some of the star athletes. I wasn't among the worthy until Jace noticed me. My first invite was the night of the fire, and despite my initial reluctance, I would have shown up, had I not ended up at the hospital.

Yuki waves her hand to the entrance, and punches in a code on a device at the side before the doors swing on their axes.

Manon follows her in, but Melina stops to look back at me. "Aren't you coming?"

"I don't have a key card yet." Jason did talk about a key card this morning, right?

She tilts her head. "Come on in, it's cold. You can wait for whoever will show you around in a game room."

"There's a game room?"

She grins from ear to ear. "Several, actually."

———

I don't know why I expected this place to look gaudy. The legacies wouldn't do gaudy if it was the only way to save humanity. They'd gladly die to preserve stylishness.

The interior is modern and simple, in dark shades of gray with gold accents.

The large entry hall could host one hell of a party, and I'm guessing it has. It is mostly empty, except for a series of comfortable black suede sofas, potted olive trees, and the occasional sculpture. There are bookshelves suspended on the walls, and the closest ones I see are packed with recent bestsellers—YA, thrillers, fantasy, the occasional romance. No school curriculum classics in sight.

Damn him, Jason was right. I do love the vibe of Glass. "Nice."

The space is bathed in natural light, and I can see the lake through the wall around the doors. To either side of me, there are several doors locked with a similar device to the one at the main entrance.

"Right?" Mel grins. "So, what do you feel like, music room, video game, home theater, VR?" She points to different doors as she lists the various forms of entertainment. "Unless you'd like a snack. Dinner's at six, but there's always tea and cake in the common rooms in the afternoon."

And to think I believed the common dorm had a sweet setup. "Err—too many choices. All of that at once, I guess?"

"That's my girl." Jason walks down a flight of floating stairs matching the black bookshelves. "Always hungry for more."

I stiffen and narrow my eyes. "I'm not your anything." He doesn't get to call me his. "You must have me confused with Marie Vaughn."

Jason reaches the brushed gray floor and chuckles. "Gosh, you're insanely jealous. It's cute."

"I'm no such thing," I grit between my teeth.

"Why, with you swearing up and down that we're nothing to each other, I don't see why you would be." He bites his lip and gives me one of the rare smiles that reach his eyes.

I could strangle him.

"Aren't you supposed to be at practice?" Jason has football every day after school.

In the mornings, he wears the school blazer like any students but after PE, he and the rest of his team gets changed into their letter jackets, reminding us that they're more important than the rest of us, I guess.

Most of our school teams suck. The soccer team's only decent player is my cousin. He's won some games for Cross, but they've never stood out in a championship.

The varsity swimming team Sophia belongs to does pretty well overall, though they don't figure in the national board.

Cross and Roses prides itself on its academic achievements more than sports.

The football team is another story. I heard the Beasts didn't use to be worth shit, but when Jason and his friends joined the school, the level considerably improved. They brought in Coach Pierson, who's supposed to be a hotshot from the NFL.

I don't give a shit about football, so I've never attended a game, but I hear they win a lot. Pierson takes the game seriously, and won't like his tight end skipping training.

"I'm supposed to do exactly what I fucking want to, doll." Jason is arrogant as ever.

He tosses something to me and I catch it on instinct. It's a black card with my initials on it, attached to a key ring shaped like crown.

"Come on. Let me give you a tour."

I stay planted, glaring at him. "I'm fine, thank you."

I need a fucking tour, or at least to know where my room is.

Jason crosses the distance between us. "So long, Melina," he says without sparing her a glance, his focus pinned on me.

"You can stay, Mel." I cross my arms over my chest. "It's your home as well as his."

And mine, too, from now on.

"Ooookay, I'll leave you guys to it." She opts to retreat, and I can't really blame her.

He reaches me and I hide the way his proximity makes me feel as best I can, refusing to back down, even when he lowers his mouth to my level.

His finger brushes against my cheek, pushing my hair back. "She means nothing, Nadia," he whispers against my ear. "No one else means anything at all. Only you."

I slap his hand away. "She means something to *me*. She means getting your nuts off is more important to you than me. And I should have known as much all along."

I don't know how long I glare at him for. I should kick him in the balls. He isn't expecting it this time; I'd hit my target.

"I wouldn't touch her if she were the last woman on earth."

"You did. I distinctly remember you touching her at lunch."

He shakes his head and laughs low. "So jealous."

I kick his shin.

"Ouch," he says lightly, visibly not even a little bit hurt. "She destroyed your work when I specifically told the school to leave you alone." He's still murmuring against my skin. I wish I didn't tingle all over. "I need to know who made her do that. And more importantly, I need to know what they'll ask her to do next, so we have the upper hand."

Oh.

Oh.

That makes a lot of sense, actually. And part of me is unsurprised, as though I expected him to have a reason all along. As though I trusted him.

Except... "And you need to fuck her to find out?"

"I already told you I'm not going there. But pretending I *could* doesn't hurt. She's more malleable that way." I hate his infuriating grin so much. "I mean, if I had a girlfriend, I wouldn't pimp myself out for the greater good, but apparently I don't, so letting her think she can get her hands on me isn't hurting anyone. Right?"

I hate him so fucking much. "Whatever, asshole. Where's my room?"

CHAPTER TWELVE

y room is ridiculous.

Five times larger than my old dorm room, and twice as large as my place at home, it's open-floorplan suite, in shades of lilac and silver. I remember Maverik asking for my favorite color. Was it to set up this space? But it was weeks ago. Jason only made me move today. It must just be a coincidence. I love it though.

My bed could comfortably host an orgy. The curtains at every corner of the see-through walls fall to the floor, black as night, luxuriant and soft-looking.

In one corner of the room, there's a desk set up over a plush circular rug, with an expensive computer perched on top. On the other end of the room, ensconced atop an elevated platform, there's a freestanding lion-claw-footed tub.

I've seen that kind of arrangement in multimillion-dollar house listings.

The metal chandelier on the high ceiling flickers between blue and green light when we walk in.

"You can control the lighting with a remote in your bedside table," Jason says, opting to turn the light off with a flick of the switch next to my door.

"This is your bathroom," he says, pointing to one of the two silver doors behind the tub. He opens the second.

"And your wardrobe."

Wardrobe is a serious understatement: it's a walk-in closet.

The contents of my suitcase are already unpacked, folded, and hung. Along with all my stuff, I note the presence of several new things.

There are at least half a dozen more uniforms than the ones I own—and I know the Cross uniform runs five hundred bucks each—but also several pairs of shoes that appear to be in my size. I note a silky red dress, and a sparkly blue one that I definitely didn't bring with me.

I wrinkle my nose. "I don't need new clothes, Jason."

"I'm aware. In case you hadn't noticed, I'm inherently selfish, Nadia. I got you new clothes because it pleased me to do so, not because I thought you needed them."

Of all the things he might have said, that might be the only answer that can make me accept his inappropriate presents.

His hands reaches out to indicate velvety, white fabric. "I want to see you wear that soon."

I lift one strappy red shoe in my hand and raise an eyebrow. "And these?"

"It would *really* please me to see you in those fuck-me heels."

I roll my eyes and put it down. "Yeah, well, I don't want to fall on my ass and snap my neck in the process, so...pass. But thank you, I guess."

"You can always *show* your thanks," he teases.

His eyes flicker with surprise as I cross over to him and get to my toes to kiss one of his cheeks, then the other.

Truth be told, I'm not thanking him for the shoes I'll never wear, or the room I didn't ask for, or the clothes I don't need. I'm kissing him because I want to. Finding out that he's around Marie not only for a specific reason, but one that's to my benefit, has melted most of my anger, and now that it's gone, all that remains is my desire.

I don't know why I take his word for it, rather than questioning whether he's lying about Marie, but I do believe him.

I press my mouth to his and lick his bottom lip. Jace growls and take control of the kiss, as I knew he would. It's hot, heavy, and over way too quickly. I grunt in protest when he tears his mouth away from mine, but before I know it, he's scooping me up. I shriek and laugh as he carries me over to the bed and dumps me onto it.

Jace hovers on top of me. "For someone who's not my girlfriend, you're enjoying my mouth a fair bit today, doll."

"You're *insanely* fascinated with being my boyfriend, Jason. *It's cute*," I say, echoing his tone from earlier.

He chuckles, unlacing my boots. "I don't want to be your boyfriend." He kicks his shoes off, and shrugs off his letter jacket. "I want to be the first thing you see when you wake up. I want my cock inside you every night as you fall asleep. I want *everything*." Jason peels his shirt off and I stare at his sculpted frame. I think I drool. "Whatever label you need to put on it, I want you to understand you're mine, deep inside, so clearly you never need to question my intentions."

He's saying words, and they make me *feel*, but if I'm telling the truth, I don't really hear him, because my mouth is watering at the sheer sight of him.

I sit up, hands reaching out to him. I need to touch him, feel him.

"Oh, no." He chuckles. "Not yet. When we touch, it tends to be over a little too quickly, and it occurred to me I've yet to see you naked. Time to remedy that."

"You're one to talk," I shoot back.

At least he's had me half naked a time or two, while I've never so much as seen his torso before. Keeping those abs to himself was downright selfish.

I'm still fully dressed, wearing my duffle coat, so perhaps he has a point. I unzip it, and shed the blazer along with it, before opening the button of my shirt.

"You remember the first time I had you on a bed, Nadia?" He pauses. "The only time, really."

"How could I forget," I reply dryly.

He made me spread my legs and touch myself—then when I failed to do it properly, he took over. I was as scared and humiliated as I was turned on.

"How about a redo?" Jason unbuckles his belt, eyes locked on me.

I want to ask what he means, but I'm too fascinated by what he's doing as he lowers his pants and boxers. His upturned cock is already rock hard, pointing straight at me. He wraps his fist around the base and pumps it once. I think I whimper.

"A redo?" I don't recognize my voice at all, it's so breathy.

"I want to watch you again. And I want you to watch me."

I lift my hips and remove my skirt and tights so fucking fast.

Whatever else goes on between us, this part? The sex? It's right. Easy. Natural.

"My god, you're so beautiful." Devouring me with his eyes, he slowly pumps his cock, up and down, and up again. "Go on. Show me."

I wish I was better at masturbating. I wish I knew how to make it look as sexy as he does. I don't, so I do what comes to mind, what feels right. I run my left hand along my breasts through my lacy bra, and lower the right one to the edge of my panties, sliding underneath.

I've never been this sensitive while touching myself before. The slightest brush reverberates through my body, electrifying my insides. I moan.

"That's right, doll. Go on. Make yourself feel good for me."

I keep touching myself. Frustrated with the layer of fabric, I lower the cups of the bra and squeeze at the small, sensitive nub.

"Jesus, Nadia, is that a tattoo on your fucking tit?"

I look down, as if surprised to see it there. "Oh, yeah. I got it last summer, when I turned eighteen."

The five butterflies dance from the center to the side of my breast, one resting right over my nipple.

"Fuck. It's so fucking hot, Nadia. Keep going. I want you to come like this. Please come for me." His wrist is moving faster, and his cock's getting impossibly bigger. I watch him wince as he struggles to retain control.

Fuck, I don't even need to touch myself, I could come just from looking at him. I rub my pussy faster under my panties and wail. It's so fucking good.

I must have said it out loud because he replies, "I know, doll. So good."

Jason folds over me and takes my mouth, sweeping his tongue inside. He swallows my groan, and then he pulls back and lowers his mouth to my neck, licking the sensitive skin there. Next he kisses along my shoulder. "Don't stop. Don't you fucking stop."

I wouldn't stop if this room caught on fire like the first one. I'm frantically wiping my pussy, hard and harsh, and touching my tits nonstop. His mouth kisses each of my butterflies before wrapping around my hard nipple.

His hands skim along my hips just as I scream out, my

entire body releasing all of its tension in one explosion of senses.

I'm panting so hard and deep.

Jason lifts his head from my breast to ask, "Are you on the pill now?"

Oh, shit. It didn't even occur to me to look into birth control with everything I had going on. And I should have. I shake my head.

He runs his hand along my stomach and then to the edges of my panties. "I have a condom in my wallet," he tells me. "But I'm not going to use it. I'm going to come inside you."

He's telling me, but he's not doing it, and I know this is his version of asking for permission. As close as Jason Alden ever gets to asking, that is. "It's risky, Jace."

We've already done it once, and it was no less risky then, but that's beside the point.

"The only risk is us making a baby. It's a little ahead of schedule, but you'd still get to graduate, and he should come right before college." He pushes the tip of his cock against my entrance. "We can get hitched as soon as my mother plans the wedding. I can make her keep the crazy to a minimum, so we'll have the ceremony within the month, before you're showing. How would you like that?" His cock runs up and down my slick, needy folds.

"We're not getting married. We're not having a child. That's insane."

"Yeah?" His tip presses harder at my core. "It'd be cute. A little like me, a little like you. We'd have a full-time nanny, naturally, so we can both go to college. I'd fuck you every single night. Every single day. That's our future." His cock enters me so slowly, filling me up. "Think about it when I fill you up."

Someone knocks at the door, and Jace smirks as his hips push forward, maddeningly slow. "Who is it?" he calls out loud.

I fight back a groan.

"Cain," the offender calls through the door. "Practice was cancelled. You guys want to watch a movie or something?"

"I have a better idea," Jason calls back. "Come in."

Oh, fuck! He didn't, right? I must have imagined those last words.

The door opens before I can say a word or even think about covering myself.

Cain strolls in, kicking the door shut and whistles.

"Jason!" I scream. "How about you, I don't know, *ask*?"

"Why would I do that? You might say no."

Jace doesn't bother to move from between my thighs as Cain walks closer to the bed.

"Cain, my pretty doll loves being watched. That's more fun than most movies, don't you think?"

"Hell fucking yes. Damn, that's a hot body you have there, cupcake. Can I sit?"

He's asking me and not Jason. To be honest, I hate being given the choice. I *want* him to sit and watch, but saying it is too fucking mortifying. Besides, I don't know what he'll do. I don't want him to touch me. At least, I don't think I do.

I look at Jason.

"You can sit, Cain. Hands off, though. You know the rule."

I don't know the rule. Nothing about what's happening here is even remotely familiar or normal to me, but I know my insides tighten in anticipation. I like this. More than I care to admit, more than I can even understand.

I want this.

"Ready?"

Am I ever.

CHAPTER THIRTEEN

J ace's entrance is excruciatingly slow and he
reaches deep. I'm dying for more. My hips lift to
meet his, and he raises up in the air, holding my
sides high and firm.

I exhale as he withdraws and inches forward again,
until our skin meets, his pace leisurely. At first, I'm staring
at his cock moving in and out of me, but I catch a glimpse
of Cain at the corner of my eyes, and I look at him
instead.

Oh, god. Jason was already so deep, but all of a
sudden, my inner folds awaken.

This feels different from when David looked at us
earlier today through the rearview mirror. David is a
stranger. This is Cain Warren, the guy who hates romance
stories and loves to send me selfies with Jason in the background just to drive me insane.

It's insanely hotter, but also flustering. I didn't even

stop to think about what the driver thought of what I looked like in the car, but I wonder if I turn Cain on. If he likes small tits like mine.

Jason's moving a little faster, but considerably deeper, the head of his cock hammering my walls over and over again. I'm breathing so hard.

"Nadia would very much like to see you rub your cock as I fuck her, Cain. Isn't that right, doll? You want my best friend to fuck himself watching you."

My eyes fly back to Jace just as he pulls out, his cum-coated cock hovering over me.

"Don't stop," I protest.

"Then answer me." His hand reaches out to my face, thumb running along my lip. "Isn't that right, Nadia? You want to watch Cain jack off to you, don't you?"

Frustrated he's no longer content with my silent lack of refusal, I nod. Thankfully, he decides that's sufficient. Jason moves both of my legs over one of his shoulders and slams back home. It's harder and faster now, and I throw my head back, taking it all.

By the time I look over again, Cain's opened his pants and pulled his cock out. It's so different from Jason's. Straight and longer, though perhaps a little thinner. Both of those boys were infinitely blessed with their assets.

"Don't look at me like that, cupcake," Cain says, rhythmically moving his hand up and down his shaft. "I can't fuck you."

I'm not asking him to fuck me. Right? I just like being watched. It's a thing. There's even a word for it.

Voyeurism. Or in my case, exhibitionism. I'm the exhibitionist and he, the voyeur. That doesn't mean I want...that.

My core tightens.

Oh, I want it. I want him to put his cock inside me and screw me just like Jason. If I close my eyes, I can see it.

What the *fuck* is wrong with me?

"Why?" I find myself asking.

Jason laughs. His next thrust comes hard, hitting so deep and fast it almost hurts. Oh, fuck. He winces and leans forward, grunting as his rhythm changes to slow, rough strokes that threaten to split me in two.

"Greedy girl. Answer her, Warren," Jace hisses. "I'm a little busy."

As his best friend screws my brains out, and while Cain wanks himself, he tells me, "Jason and I go way back, cupcake. And we want to keep that relationship. That means avoiding complications. Me fucking his woman? Complicated. Now, when I have someone myself, we can all play together." He bites his lip as his fist moves faster. "Would you like that, cupcake? Me fucking you while Jason screws my wife?"

God, yes.

"That will only happen once I have an attachment of my own. To ensure we don't get our feelings messed up."

I want to tell him I don't have any feelings for him, and that's actually true. I mean, I like Cain. I don't trust him much, but I like him. He's fun, and he was trying to keep me updated when I was away. That was nice. But he doesn't wreak havoc on my insides. I don't think of him unless he's in front of me. We're literally just friends. Not even that. Friendly. And if he weren't here right now, with his cock out, as I'm getting fucked faster and faster, I'd never even consider thinking about him as a sexual partner.

I can't say all that because I'm too busy moaning, panting, and curling my toes.

"You..." I managed. "Last summer. All of you we— were screwing some girl."

Jason's grunt morphs into a throaty snicker. "Some girl. Not *my* woman." He curses and lowers his mouth to mine, his thrusts growing frantic. His kiss is hot and deep and over all too soon. Jason peels his face from mine to turn to Cain.

"Did you know my gorgeous doll isn't on the pill?"

"Holy shit." His voice sounds throaty, bringing my attention to him.

"It's my second time fucking her bare. The first didn't take. This one might. Wouldn't you like that, Nadia?"

"No, I would not!" I say, determined.

"And yet you let me fuck you raw, so you're not entirely against it, are you doll?"

I've never even considered children, and if I had, it wouldn't be something I'd think about *now*. Maybe we can have kids in ten years. Or twenty.

Something hits me then.

We.

I thought "we," as in Jason and I. Not me with some random guy I'll meet in the future. I can imagine the two of us clearly, screwing, and laughing, and fighting, and screwing some more.

That's the first time I understand what he's been trying to tell me for a while. That he sees it too, that remote future where I'm still with him. His.

"Jason!" It's too much. He's found a spot so intense I could black out, and the head of his cock keeps pummeling it.

"Almost, doll. Hold it for just a few more moments."

"I…" Holy shit. I scream. "Can't."

"You can. Come with me. Just a little longer."

I wouldn't have thought it possible, but he's getting faster and deeper and I think, bigger too. I've crossed the threshold of pleasure and moved into pain, yet somehow, I want more, more, more.

"Now. Come with me *now*."

I explode around him, tears in my eyes, and losing all sense of where, or even who I am.

Other than his.

CHAPTER FOURTEEN

Cain soon excuses himself to go clean up, as he's come all over his hand and his pants. He doesn't return.

I don't know how long I stay in bed with Jason. I don't think I can move and if I could, I wouldn't want to.

This is nice. Uncomplicated. Neither of us talks, probably unwilling to get back to reality for a little longer. The reality where I still have a psycho after me because of my involvement with him. The reality where I have to end things.

My stomach grumbles, unceremoniously interrupting the comfortable silence.

"I guess we did use up a fair bit of energy," Jace chuckles. "Let's order some food."

It turns out, we can order room service through an app developed just for Glass. They have a dining room on the ground floor, but they don't have to eat there unless they want to.

"How much are you guys paying to board here?" I muse.

I wince, imagining Uncle Lucius getting the bill.

"Nothing—well, no more than any other student. Glass is a family perk."

"Of course it is. No one gets better deals than wealthy folks who don't need them."

"Hey, less with the hate on wealthy folk, doll." Jason kisses my temple. "You're one of them."

"Hardly."

"You're heir to half of your uncle's fortune," he reminds me. "That's a fair chunk of change."

I wrinkle my nose.

Jason first dropped that bombshell a few days before the fire, and I did mention it to Uncle Lucius while I was at the hospital. He was rather unconcerned. "Who else would I give it to? Lucas doesn't need all of it, and you know I love you. We're family."

It seemed rather straightforward when said that way, but I'm still on the fence about the whole thing. I don't know how clean his business is. What if I get in trouble by association? What if the extended "family" on the Astrella side starts paying attention to me?

"Besides, you could have a little Alden in there right now, and he's worth billions."

I swat his arm. I seriously need to get on the pill. "Stop being silly. I'm *not* going to get pregnant."

Hopefully. Gosh, why the fuck didn't I tell him to put his fucking condom on?

I lost all of my braincells the moment I saw him shirtless, that's why.

"Haven't heard that for a while."

His tone is a little strange, so I glance up at Jason, and find him staring at my ceiling. "Hm?"

"Stop being silly. When I was growing up, Alex kept telling me that. He was the serious one, the overachiever. I made jokes and didn't take anything too seriously."

I almost tease him, asking what happened for him to become what he is now, but thankfully, I catch myself before I do.

I know what happened. His twin was murdered. I saw the aftermath firsthand.

"Jokes," I repeat. "You know jokes?"

I can't picture it.

"I used to," he says, though he sounds unsure, as though that past, that part of himself, is unfamiliar. "They don't appeal to me anymore."

"You don't say." I'm entirely unsurprised. He laughs, sometimes, but it's typically directed at someone. "What's the best thing about Switzerland?"

"Fondue," he replies, and he's probably right. It's rather hard to beat melted cheese.

"You're not supposed to give a real answer. You're supposed to ask '*what?*'."

"What?" he parrots obediently.

"I don't know, but the flag is a big plus." I don't know

many jokes, and this one is particularly lame, but it's the first that came to mind. "Never trust atoms. They make up everything."

In my opinion, that one was superior, but Jason says, "I will literally pay you to stop."

I giggle, racking my brain for something else. "Why does a mermaid wear seashells? Because she outgrew her B-shells!"

"If I have to put something in your mouth to shut you up, I'm more than happy to do so."

Like that's a deterrent. I should be all sexed out for a least a week, but the semi-veiled threat awakens my body.

A sharp knock at my door interrupts me before I can think of a knock-knock joke.

"Perfect timing." Jace's only wearing boxers, and doesn't care one bit. He goes to open the door.

A woman in a sharp black suit, with a crisp white shirt hold up two silver platters. He takes both and closes the door in her face without a word.

"Rude," I say. "You could tip or say thank you."

"She's a Heritage employee, and she makes six figures for a very easy job. She doesn't need a tip, or a thank you."

"You're a terrible person. Why do I like you?"

"Hormones and chemistry, mostly." He grins unapologetically. "Plus, you're inexorably attracted to power, and I have that in spades."

I glare at him, hating him for thinking that. I don't care about his power, or his money. He's right about chemistry, and probably about hormones too, but my fascination with him started way before those kicked in. I noticed him at his brother's funeral because he seemed sad, and cold, and empty, and I wanted to fix it. When we met again, my eyes were following him before I knew his name.

This thing between us started for all the wrong reasons. If it wasn't for that day at the cemetery, he would never have noticed me. I'm not his type. He'd be more than happy to stick to his plan to get hitched to Yuki. And it would be more normal, healthier.

"Don't make that face. I'm just teasing you. Dinner, then I'll actually finish that tour I offered."

"I don't need a tour," I say. "I've seen where my room is, I'll figure out the rest. You don't have to stay."

He holds my stare before sighing, one hand running through his silky hair. "You know I like games as much as anyone, but I'm getting tired of this one, Nadia."

"I'm not playing," I mutter, frustrated with myself and him. "I was clear from the start." Letting him do whatever he wanted to me today probably didn't help getting my point across, though. "It's dangerous for me to be with you, when some psycho's happy to kill me to prevent that."

His tight jaw ticks, but after a long moment, he says, "Okay. Fine. But I take care of the problem and you stop this nonsense, are we clear?"

I frown. "It's hardly nonsense. I'm talking about staying alive."

"Are we clear?"

I watch him for seconds, before bobbing my head up and down.

The smile he shoots me leaves me rather uneasy. What exactly have I agreed to here?

CHAPTER FIFTEEN

I sleep like a rock. The bed is incredibly comfortable, and the orgasms certainly help.

In the morning, I somewhat regret not taking up Jason's offer for a tour, because I have no idea where the dining room Mel told me about is located. I put on my uniform, bypass the brand-new shoes in favor of my trusty old Docs, and arm myself with my headphones before heading out, bag dangling off one shoulder.

"Hey, cupcake."

There are only three boys using that stupid nickname, now that Jace has moved on to "doll." I'm not entirely certain which one's calling me until I turn around. "Rowan."

The object of young Monique's inappropriate fantasies jogs up to me. "Didn't know you were on our floor!" He grins and points to the left. "I'm three doors down on the other side, in case you need anything."

The hospitality is rather uncharacteristic, so I'm suspicious. "Why would I need anything?"

I find myself flushing. Did Jace and Cain tell him about yesterday? Is that why he thinks I'd go to his room?

He shrugs. "I hear you suck so bad in Calculus, you might fail. Wouldn't want that. If you have a question, you could buzz me."

"You're offering to tutor me?" I've entered another dimension, that's the only explanation I can think of. "Why? What's in it for you?"

He laughs easily. "Look, I've never hidden the fact that I'm an asshole, but Jason moved you here. That means something. He's in it for the long haul. And, well, over the long haul, say I need to ask a favor—it wouldn't hurt to have a pretty lady reminding him that I helped her pass her math requirements, now, would it?"

I gape, astonished. "Why... Are you guys capable of doing anything at all without treating it like a business decision?"

"I'm not much for planning ahead, actually." Rowan shrugs. "Might as well enjoy ourselves now, since you never know what will happen in the future. I don't do anything unless I want to."

Shit. All of a sudden, I remember that Rowan's parents are dead. I don't know much about them, how old they were, what happened, but I feel like an asshole, so I backtrack. "It's really nice of you to offer. And I do suck at calc. Missing a month didn't help. If you don't mind running me through the derivatives nonsense, I'd be grateful, actually."

He bobs his head, his shoulder-length, impossibly bouncy blond hair moving like he's in a conditioner commercial. "You got it. This afternoon after practice?"

"Thanks. And would you mind letting me know where the dining room is? I should have breakfast." I'm not particularly hungry, after the feast I gorged on last night, but I know I'll regret it before lunch if I don't eat something.

"Heading there myself. Come along, young padawan."

"You're such a nerd." I would have never guessed before I knew him, despite the rockstar-worthy hair. He's a jock, through and through. Quarterback of the football team, always hanging out with cheerleaders, wearing his letter jacket all the time, but the guy can't stop quoting *Star Wars*.

"What I am is disappointed. You don't even have any scars. Definitely not Vader worthy." He grimaces, leading us to the staircase. "To hear Jason talk, you'd think you were burnt more than marshmallow at a bonfire."

I lift my palm to his eye level. "This is as bad as it gets."

He winces at the sight of the mangled skin at the center of the palms. "That must have hurt."

"Like a bitch." I tried to open my door and metallic handle was scorching hot. "But the rest of the burns healed up fine, I shouldn't have scars. The worst of the damage was my hair, really."

"I like the new style." His hand threads through my hair and shakes my head affectionately. "Okay, so the ground floor only includes communal areas—your key fob will open any of the doors. On the right, you have entertainment. On the left, you have the essentials: food," he says, pointing to the door closest to the stairs. "Laundry, and the last room goes to security. One of the guards is always on call. If you forget or lose your key, you can contact them at the door by pressing zero four times on the entry keypad. Got it?"

He speaks so fast I only really assimilate half of the information, but before I can double-check anything, he opens the dining hall and strolls inside.

Whatever I expected, it wasn't the vibe of a trendy five-star restaurant with an open kitchen. "What the hell?"

He grins. "Not bad, right?"

"Is that a bar? Why is there a bar in a school dorm?"

I follow him to an oval table covered in pristine white cloth.

"They only serve mocktails, naturally." He winks and sit down.

"Naturally," I echo, completely stunned.

A server appears shortly with a menu.

A freaking menu.

"We're running a little late. Two breakfast burritos to go?" Rowan asks me.

When I nod, he hands both menus back to the server.

I figured I might not find anyone to catch a ride with, so I got up fifteen minutes earlier than usual to account for the walk to the U. I actually thought I was early, for my standards, but that was before I knew I would have breakfast somewhere that deserves a Michelin star.

I notice the room is almost empty. The legacies must eat earlier to take full advantage of this place. "This is ridiculous, you realize that?"

"I mean, sure, I guess, but only when you consider Glass a dorm. It isn't—not really. Glass is directly owned by our parents' club, not by the school. So, it would stand to reason that it's managed differently."

"Nothing about this stands to reason. We're teenagers. We don't need to eat fancy shit every single day."

Rowan chuckles. "Who said anything about needs?"

Our server's already back with two brown paper bags. "I took the liberty of adding water, sir, miss."

"Thanks dude," Rowan says, standing to grab both bags. "Come on, I'll give you a lift. We can eat in the car."

Our breakfast is full of flavor, but I notice several tastes I would never have added in there, like roasted asparagus. It's delicious, and much healthier than a burrito has any business being. No wonder the legacies are all fit if their nutrition is managed like this.

Rowan's driver gets us up to school much earlier than I usually arrive. I notice plenty of eyes watching me climb out of the back of his Audi, and I inwardly sigh. Great. Now that's going to feed the rumor mill for a while.

"Thanks for the tour. And the lift. And, you know, the tutoring." That's three more thanks than I would have imagined giving to Rowan White before today.

"Any time, cupcake."

I drop my books in my locker before dragging my feet to Calculus.

"So, are you and Rowan an item?" some girl I've never talked to asks the moment I sit down. I think she's called Verona. "Is that why they moved you to Glass?"

The first bell rings.

"No."

She doesn't seem deterred by my visible lack of interest. "To which question?"

"Both," I say tersely, putting my headphones on, though I don't turn on the music.

I just want her, and the rest of the wolves, to leave me alone.

CHAPTER SIXTEEN

I arrive first in literature, and when Jason walks in with Cain, he just nods at me in polite greeting before taking a seat toward the back.

I hate it.

The problem with making rational decisions is that they rarely align with what we truly want to do.

Melina sits next to me, and babbles cheerfully about her upcoming London trip, thankfully not requiring much input from me.

We're still watching TV today, so my attention isn't required. I pretend to take notes, but end up doodling all over the page instead. I can always watch the show later anyway.

When class is over, I glance at Jason as I pack up my stuff. He leaves without so much as a glance.

I asked for this. I even convince myself I wanted it.

I'd like to say I take his indifference better as time

passes, but it hurts as much the next day, and the day after that. A week later, I'm still not used to it.

It's not like he pretends I don't exist. He says hi every day, polite as ever.

I'm no longer having a terrible time at Cross. The mob is leaving me alone, Glass makes it seem like I'm on a long-term all-inclusive holiday, and even my calculus grade improves. Lucas is at school most days, too, and nothing much happens to me. My doctor's visit confirms that I am blissfully not pregnant, and my STD scan comes back all clear—two blessings, given my stupid recent behavior. I get an implant, rather than opting for the kind of contraception I could forget to take or renew.

Everything is fine.

For all that, I'm miserable. I can't even pretend otherwise.

Two weeks later, I ask Jace if he had fun in London, as Mel couldn't stop talking about their trip. Nothing Heritage-specific, but she chats nonstop about the cool people she met and the awesome clothes she bought.

"It was fine, thank you, Nadia."

Nadia. Fucking *Nadia*, not doll, not cupcake. I could scream.

I often eat with Melina at Glass, when I don't opt to order room service. She and I are becoming fast friends, though we certainly have our differences. From time to time, Judith Cushman joins us. She and Melina get along just fine, and seem to know each other quite well, but there's a fair bit of tension between the two.

Melina's the kind of social butterfly who's accepted wherever she goes. She hangs out with Yuki, Jacqueline, and the It Girls, with some underclassmen, with the boys, with *me*, her friendly nature welcome in every circle. Yet when she's around Judith, there's an edge to her words.

At the start of February, after she shoots Judith a particularly frosty look during dinner, I ask Mel what's their deal on our way to our bedrooms.

"Jude is fine," she replies tightly.

I snort. "Right. That was convincing."

Melina sighs. "I'm not a gossip, Nadia. People like me because they know their shit stays private with me."

"I'm not a gossip either. I just wonder why there's some tension between two of my friends," I reply reasonably. "But if you'd rather not say, no worries."

Mel hesitates, then opens her bedroom door. "Fine. Come on in."

My eyebrows twitch up an inch. She's never invited me into her bedroom before.

I walk into a space that looks nothing like mine, except that it's the same size. The walls are painted black, and completely covered. There are two guitars, several posters, and rows upon rows of books everywhere.

Her bed is covered with a red comforter and black pillows.

I always see Melina in uniform, so I never realized she was quite this fond of metal stuff. I suppose she tends to paint her nails black or bloodred, but she's hardly the only one.

"I like what you did with the place."

"Really?" She's genuinely surprised. "I thought you were more into, I don't know, princessy stuff."

"Princessy?" That's how she sees me?

"You know, frills, pink, whatever."

"I like rollerblading and I saw Transcendence in concert last summer," I say, pointing to one of her posters, showing a group of four hot guys who took the alternative rock world by storm two years ago. "Not that there's anything wrong with pink. I'll pass on frills though."

Mel grins. "You know Transcendence is a Heritage group, right?"

My jaw falls. "Shut up."

She walks to a fluffy rug and sits on it. "Yeah, they're thorns and stems. Tons of celebrities only make it because they're in the club."

"Thorns and stems?" I echo, joining her.

"You don't know much, do you?" She rolls her eyes. "Boys never think to give us the information we need. Did he at least get you to sign the NDA?"

I nod. "Yeah, before talking to me about his club."

"Good. Well, there are essentially two ways of joining the Heritage. You're either a legacy, and you're in because of your parents, or you're recruited. When we recruit a guy, he's considered a thorn until he's a full member of the club. Then he's a stem. For the girls, they're petals, then blossoms. That lingo is only used for us juveniles. They drop the appellations once we hit thirty. We're just members, then."

"So, you're a...blossom?" I guess.

"No, I'm a legacy. You're essentially a petal, though. Or you will be once Jason officially initiates you."

"Initiates," I repeat with a sneer. "It sounds like a cult."

"I mean, religion has nothing to do with the Heritage, so not really, but it operates in secrecy, and to the world, we pretend to be a simple private club into philanthropy, so it's not the worst analogy."

"So the members of Transcendence were recruited?"

She bobs her head. "Yep. The Heritage picks exceptional people and helps them reach their potential. You wouldn't believe the number of actors and singers we've sponsored. Anyway, back to Judith. We used to be super close, but she's been on a downward spiral for a while. I don't have anything against her. I'm just worried for her."

I remember what Judith told me at the start of the year—that she'd been buying drugs at Jason's club. "Spiraling how?"

"Self-destructions of various types. Too much alcohol, drugs, shopping. She barely even studies—her mom bribes the teachers so she passes her classes. Her mother took her credit cards over the summer, and she's been fucking guys for money to finance her habits since."

I wouldn't have been more shocked if she'd told me Judith was a pig in a dress. "Prostitution?" That makes no sense to me. "I mean, she comes from a wealthy family. Why would she..."

"Because she wants to do what she wants, and her mother won't let her. She's inherently spoiled. I mean, we all are. I don't know what I'd do if my parents cut me off. Which they won't. They don't care the way Lara Cushman does."

I'm constantly reminded that the legacies are from another universe, but this takes the cake. "You wouldn't sell yourself."

Mel shrugs. "I mean, it's not like she's fucking just anyone. She chooses guys she wants, mostly from Cross, and she lets them know she'll blow them for a hundred bucks, or whatever. I think she enjoys it. That's not why I'm worried. It's the drugs. She's taking more and more, and the kind of people who sell them to her aren't safe, Nadia."

No fucking shit. "Is there any way you can help her? Tell her mom to send her to rehab or something?"

"She's eighteen. No one can make her do anything. Cutting her off only pushed her closer to the edge. So, anyway, that's my issue with Judith. I don't like watching her hurt herself."

We're sitting in silence, my thought directed toward the gorgeous, seemingly carefree social butterfly who helped me pass chem lab junior year, when someone knocks at Melina's door.

She pushes up to her feet and opens the door. "What?" she says, clearly put out.

"You agreed to help, Mel." I'd recognize that voice anywhere. "You're not dressed like you remember that."

I turn to the door, and frown at finding Jason leaning in the door frame, like there's nothing more natural than for him to be in front of Melina's room.

She sighs. "I lost track of the time. Give me ten."

Jason's gaze slides away from her, over to me.

He stares at me as though he doesn't like what he's seeing. Like I don't belong here.

Yeah, well, I'm not particularly happy to see him either.

"Nadia."

"Jason," I reply, jaw tight.

He redirects his glare to Mel, who sighs again. "She had questions. About Judith, actually. And a lot of other stuff I shouldn't be the one telling her."

Jason looks back at me for a long while before straightening up and shoving his hands back in his pockets.

"Ten minutes, Mel."

CHAPTER SEVENTEEN

I'm going to explode and it won't be pretty.

"Jason, slow the fuck down!" Mel shouts from the back of my bike.

At least I think that's what she shouts. Not that it fucking matters. I don't care what she's saying, after the shit she pulled tonight.

She *knows* how fucking close I am to losing it, and she's still rubbing all over Nadia like she belongs to her.

She doesn't. She's mine.

Mine, mine, *mine*.

If Melina wants to fuck my woman, she'll do it on *my* terms.

"Dammit, Jason!" she yells. "You know I'm not moving on your fucking girlfriend. Slow down before you kill both of us!"

I'm an excellent driver, though admittedly, I'm in no state to push my bike this fast tonight.

I haven't been for a month.

I slow down a little, because it's not really Melina I'm raging against. Keeping my distance from Nadia is a fucking nightmare. She hates it, I hate it. But she demanded it of me, again and again, and therefore I have to try. If only so she can finally admit that's a terrible idea and never make either of us go through it again.

If you love something, let it go, right?

I need to punch whoever said that in the teeth.

We approach the city at high speed, and I head straight to Midnight Elite. I would have preferred not to do this on a weeknight, but the moment I received the text, I moved the pieces of my trap into place.

Judith's here. And if Judith is here, then her dealer isn't far. She wouldn't come all the way to the city on a random Wednesday if it wasn't to get her supply of coke and ecstasy.

I drop Mel off a few yards away from the entrance before circling back to drive my bike down the underground entrance reserved for Heritage guests. The general public isn't aware of the basement, and we like it that way.

I rush to the room where security surveys every inch of my club.

Lucas Astrella stands in front of a dozen monitors, his keen eyes seemingly taking everything in at once.

"Where is she?" I demand, asking him rather than the two guards seated by the console.

"The shitters," he says, grinning. "Your friend's a piece of work. It's her third client."

I follow his gaze to one of the screens. Judith is busy making the money she needs to inject and snort her way into an early grave, bent over the men's urinal.

"Are you recording?"

"Yes, sir," one of the guards replies. "We've zoomed in and adjusted the lighting to ensure we have a clear shot, too."

I remember a time when little Jude ran around my parent's swimming pool, screaming "you can't catch me, you can't catch me."

I always caught her.

"Good. Has she made contact with anyone else, anyone other than her johns?"

"No, sir. She headed straight for the bathrooms."

I look at every camera, trying to decipher anything unusual, but all I see are young, beautiful people dancing, drinking, fucking, and having an all-around good time.

"Wait," Lucas says. "Zoom in on Judith and her guy."

I grimace distastefully. "We're not here for you to get an eyeful of her cunt, Astrella."

"I'm not turned on by STD magnets, asshole. Zoom in."

My guard looks to me for guidance, so I nod. There's a reason I brought Astrella onboard. His father's company consistently delivers, and he's one of their sharpest agents.

All I see is some guy in white jeans and a red leather jacket fucking Judith's ass, but Lucas nods. "That's him."

"What makes you think that?"

"Every other guy queued until it was their turn, then gave her money, and started to fuck her, no exceptions. He walked right in there and cut the line. I also didn't see him hand her any money."

"How did you even notice him?" the guard asks in awe.

"I can see patterns as easily as other people see shapes and colors. When something goes against the pattern, I notice." Lucas leans in. "See the tattoo on his ass?"

My eyes narrow, and indeed, he has a spiderweb right on his buttock. "Is that a gang tattoo?"

"Several in town use spiderwebs. He might have other, more distinctive ones to clarify where he's from. Watch them. We'll see an exchange."

So we watch the cheap porn-like session in silence, as my cameras aren't equipped with microphones. That would be useless with the deafening music.

I grab my phone and tell Mel to stand close to those bathrooms. Through the camera, I see her take her drink and move into place. Now that she's removed the biking overpants and jacket she had on while riding from Cross, she's wearing a tight glittery jumpsuit that dips so low between her tits it makes her average rack look indecent. Her platinum-blonde wig almost seems natural—as well it should. It cost me a thousand bucks.

She did well. I should be nicer to her. Too bad I've run out of nice for the time being.

I should most definitely tip Lucas Astrella, because after the spider ass-tattooed guy nuts, Judith indeed slips something in his jacket, and he puts his hands between her tits, no doubt shoving her drugs in her bra.

I text Mel to stand at the ready.

Judith moves from the urinal to the sinks, certainly aching after staying on her knees for so long. She sits and waves her next john forward. I ignore her, following the red jacket as he walks out of the bathroom.

I watch Mel bump into him, biting her lips and playing with her hair. She gets to her tiptoes and whisper in his ears. If she followed the plan, she told him Judith recommended him.

He glances back toward the bathroom suspiciously. Then she takes another step forward, pushing her tits to his chest.

"She got him. The locator's on his jacket. Damn, the girl is good. If she's looking for a job, tell her to come to me."

"Her trust fund's worth more than your father's entire company, punk."

I'm grinning, relieved the encounter went as planned.

I've tried to catch this snake for months, and failed. My next stop would have been asking my father for help, and I was determined to avoid that. Our parents want us to prove we can take care of our own shit. He would have fixed it for me, I'm sure, but he would also have made me pay for it.

Mel pays for her drugs and retreats toward the bar, not before sending an air kiss to her mark.

One problem fixed—or at least, it will be, as soon as Lucas contacts his more unsavory acquaintances to ensure that the gang stays the hell away from my club. And the threat of releasing that recording will be enough to keep Judith in check under my roof moving forward.

Now, if only all my issues could be as easily sorted out.

I hesitate, shooting a glance to Lucas. He's too close to this. But without him, I would never have noticed that there was something different about the latest guy to fuck Judith. Asking him to help me figure out who wants to hurt Nadia makes sense. If anything, he'll be even more motivated to get to the bottom of this.

"How would you feel about doing another job for me?"

"This one off the books, too?"

"Completely off the books." I consider my approach. Tilting my head, I invite him to follow me out of the room. We don't need an audience for this. "Someone's targeting your sister."

That gets his undivided attention.

"What, am I still supposed to pretend Nadia's just your cousin? That Lucius's gay-as-fuck brother impregnated the bombshell ballerina?" I shrug. "It's obvious."

"If you've guessed as much, you probably know why she's legally my cousin, and why she should continue to believe it."

Yeah, right. "Because your family's inherently sexist and your father believes she can't handle having a target on her back—though he's more than happy to let you shoulder the burden." I chuckle. "It's honestly not my problem, but if she asks, she'll get nothing but the truth from me. Thankfully for you, she doesn't suspect a thing."

Lucas doesn't seem bothered one way or another. "You said she was targeted. The fire wasn't accidental, was it?"

I nod my agreement. "She used to play with the cat that was beheaded right before."

Something flashes in his dark eyes, and for one moment, he looks exactly like his father. "And since then?"

I wrinkle my nose. "Nothing. But whoever did that, they're not afraid to punch hard. The next time they could hit the mark."

Lucas shakes his head. "Not gonna happen. I'll tell Dad to get her out of Cross."

I don't fucking think so.

I know threats aren't likely to work on Lucas *or* his father, so I appeal to his reason instead. "Whoever did that to her has a serious boner against her. We know they're part of the school. We can contain, observe, and control the environment before they get to her again. If she's in the city, or in college later, what are the chances we'll be able to catch them?"

Lucas doesn't like any of this, I can tell. Still, he considers it, because he knows I'm right. "All right, what have you tried so far?"

"You know I had Nadia moved to Glass," I say just as we reach my bike. I have to wait for Mel, but I couldn't have that chat in the control room. "Once she's out of there, a team of guards follow her at a distance. In school, one of the few friends I trust have their eyes on her at all times. I kept my distances." To my great annoyance. "Whoever it is, they seem triggered by my paying attention to her and I don't want to push them."

Lucas chuckles. "And let me guess, nothing's happened?"

I sigh. "I can't use her like bait, Lucas." It did occur to me that protecting her wasn't going to make catching whoever's after her easy.

"I'm not saying you should. By all means, ensure she's as protected as possible. I'll put my own guys on her too. But if the psycho after her is triggered by *you*, it's you who needs to provoke them."

That doesn't sound like the worst idea.

And more importantly, his plan gives me an excuse to get close to my girl again.

Whether she likes it or not.

CHAPTER EIGHTEEN

I barely sleep all night, but at least by morning, I've come to a decision. I stroll to lit class determined. Why would I freak out about what Jason could possibly do with my friend when I can just ask her?

I raced here so fast, I'm one of the first to arrive— mostly because Italian isn't very far from English. I take one of my favorite seats, dead center.

When Melina arrives, she looks exhausted, bags under her eyes, hunched over and dragging her feet. "Damn. Long night?"

She wrinkles her nose. "You have no idea."

Glad for the natural opening, I ask, "You do anything fun?"

"I mean, kinda. I had to go to Midnight Elite with Jason. I'm sure he'll tell you all about it."

There. Being mature and just asking about what's on my mind does pay off. Although I still don't have a straight answer, and I sincerely doubt Jason will tell me anything except "hi."

The man walks in, gorgeous as ever, as if summoned by my thoughts. Cain's not on his heels for once.

I shift my attention to my notebook. We're—blissfully—almost at the end of *Wuthering Heights*.

When the chair next to me scrapes over the floor, I have to glance up.

I meet Jason's gray eyes and he smiles at me. "Hi, doll."

Oh, he didn't.

Jaw tight, I keep my eyes on the empty blackboard, though Mr. Green isn't even in the room.

He leans back in his chair, and I can feel the heat of his stare. "What, aren't you going to say hi back to me?"

I don't say a single word.

My anger is rather irrational, given the fact that he's done nothing but what I demanded of him, but I didn't ask for him to pretend like we were nothing at all. And all of a sudden, I'm *doll* again? Fuck him.

Mr. Green uncharacteristically arrives at the first bell and we dissect this shitty book for an hour and a half. I suppose that's the issue with advanced placement classes: we go deeper. And when the subject sucks, it's not a lot of fun.

Time crawls until the end of the lesson, and I pack my notebook fast so I can make my escape. I smile at Mel, and rush to get to the cafeteria, ignoring Jason as best I can, though I feel his gaze.

"Congratulations!" Alexander beams.

"That's amazing, Willow," Elisa echoes as I sit at my usual table.

"What's amazing?"

My friend grins. "I got early admission to Stanford with a full ride."

"Oh my god!" I squeal, as excited as everyone else. "You're amazing. Is that your first choice?"

She nods. "Yeah, my sister's back in Cali, and, you know, it's home. I always planned on moving back. I tried Harvard and Yale, but no news yet. How about you?"

I snort. "Well, no early admissions for me."

We're chatting about college applications, and I feel as if I can finally breathe for the first time this morning.

We're eating curry, one of my favorites from the cafeteria, though I'm far less enthused about the food here after a month of dining at Glass. I'm halfway done with my plate when Jason and Cain walk over, as though it's the most natural thing in the world.

"Room for me?" he asks Willow, and she gives me a look.

At my nod, she slides over and Jace sits next to me. Cain claims a seat next to Elisa, on the opposite side. She practically hyperventilates. Not that I can blame her. These boys are a sight to behold.

Jace acts like his coming over is all perfectly normal. "So where are you applying, Nadia?" he asks.

He must have overheard some of our conversation.

I clench my jaw, keeping my mouth shut.

He whispers, "You're ignoring me again. You know I don't like that."

"Too bad. I don't care," I hiss.

His eyes flash, and then he swoops in, pressing his lips to mine. The kiss is demanding, his hand behind my neck, not giving me an escape.

Slowly, Jason draws back, and I do my best to not show any signs of being affected.

What the hell? We talked about this. He's supposed to leave me alone, and all of a sudden, he's kissing me publicly, in front of the entire senior class?

"I'm probably headed to Harvard," Cain says casually, as though the situation's entirely normal. "That's where my parents graduated from, so they're putting pressure on me to go there. I want to be with Jason, though."

I try to focus on Cain since he's talking, but Jason keeps staring at me, his hand light on my shoulder. I don't want to answer him here, so I shift my gaze to my friends, pleading with my eyes for them to say something, anything.

I have so many words for Jason, but I'll shout them at him in public later.

"I want in NYU," Elisa says. "I'll pass on the stress of an Ivy League school. The university's great anyway, and I want to be in the city." She smiles at me. "We can hang out then. I'd love to meet the friends you always talk about. Especially Gabriella."

"They're great," Jason says. "Harper and Spencer need to sort their shit out, though." To me, he says, "So you're staying in the city?"

"You don't know where she's going?" Willow asks, eyebrows raised.

"Well, I'm not officially going anywhere, Ms. Early Admittance."

She laughs. "Tisch would be stupid not to accept you. I've seen the art you sent them. You'll get in."

I wish I had her confidence in me. I also wish she hadn't told Jason exactly what he wanted to know.

Jace finally turns away from me. "Let's apply to Brown and Columbia. Harvard's cliché," he tells Cain.

Somehow, Jace's plan and opinion don't surprise me at all.

The rest of the table joins in the conversation, my friends seemingly more at ease with the invasion of the guys now, but I stay silent. I'm still reeling from that unexpected kiss, and from his touch.

What game is he playing?

I know there's a game. There always is with Jason Alden.

CHAPTER NINETEEN

I usually walk to PE with Willow, but when we're all done with our lunch, I look at her apologetically before glaring at Jason. "You don't mind if we have a quick chat?"

By chat, I mean that I'm about to scream at him for five minutes straight, and he must know it, yet he seems completely at ease. "Of course, doll."

I clear my tray and leave the cafeteria without checking if he's following, anger and confusion churning inside me. What is he up to now?

I've only exited the revolving doors when I turn on my heels and stab my finger against his hard chest. "What the hell was that, Alden? You're supposed to leave me the fuck alone."

"And I have, for a whole fucking month," he reminds me. "How did you like it, *Reyes?*"

I hated it, but that's beside the point. "I liked not being set on fire."

He rolls his eyes, nonchalantly throwing his arm around my shoulder and leading the way toward the gym. "See, I see your point, I really do. The issue is, if no one's trying to set you on fire, I have little chance of catching them."

My jaw opens and stays that way for a good long while. "What the fuck? Seriously, what the hell. You want to lure a psycho in, dangling me like a carrot in front of them until they snap?"

"When you say it that way, it sounds bad."

"Because it is." I shrug his arm off my shoulder. "I don't want to end up in the hospital again—or worse!"

"You won't." He's adamant, confident as ever, like he controls everything. But if he did, we wouldn't be in this situation.

"I'm not taking that chance, Jason."

"Oh, but you will. Now, next year, in five years. Do you truly think that someone willing to snuff you out is going to give up after we leave Cross?" We don't pass many students in the hall this close to the start of the next period, but his voice is low, so I doubt they can hear our conversation. "Someone this determined to make sure we're not together is going to crack sooner or later. If they do it here and now, I can control the situation. I have eyes everywhere, following you at all times. It's much safer to let things play out here."

It's not that I don't understand his reasoning, I just

don't agree it's worth the risk. "Maybe you should just stay away from me, in that case."

He stops, and takes my wrist to make me face him. Then his hand moves to my chin, soft as ever. "You want to give up on this?" His eyes search mine. "On us?"

I try to look away, but his fingers push my face up higher, firmer now. "I don't want to be hurt again. I don't want to *die*." And he can't afford to lose someone else either. To risk losing whatever shred of humanity is left in him. Jason's cold and detached most of the time. He barely lets anyone in. He would never have seen me if I hadn't made him at his brother's funeral. He can't endure another loss. I won't let him.

"You could cross the road and be hit by a car tomorrow."

"Sure, but goading a psycho is more like willingly crossing the highway on foot."

"I'll keep you safe, Nadia."

I huff, losing steam, because arguing with him is a headache. He's not one to change his mind, whatever I say, however reasonable I am. "Like you did that night?" I know my words are a slap in the face, but he needs to hear them. "You're not all powerful."

"I didn't know anyone was after you before. I should have protected you regardless. I'm sorry."

Jason doesn't often apologize—make that never. I know it must have cost him to admit to something he considers a failure, so I sigh and take a step toward him, my hand pressing to his chest. "It wasn't your fault. I mean, it might have happened because of you, but you are not responsible for my safety. *I* am. And I've decided to put it first." He deserves the truth, so I say it. "I hate that we have to be apart, Jace. Truly. I hate when you say hi and nothing else to me. I hate that you don't ever look at me or touch me. But you know what I'd hate more? Getting hurt, and you losing it because you'll know—and you *will* know—we could have prevented it by doing things my way."

He wordlessly closes his eyes. As seconds trickle by, I think I actually got through to him. He's coming to terms with my decision. Right?

"No."

He moves my hand from his chest and slams me against the nearest row of lockers, before taking my mouth in a ravenous, all-consuming kiss.

"Jason," I manage on a shaky breath.

He growls against my lips and sweeps me off my feet, pulling my legs around his waist. I can feel his hard length right against me through our clothing. He pushes his hips up, rubbing against me through our clothes, and tearing a long grunt from my throat.

I push against his chest, knowing he's kissing me because he's making a point. A point I'm fully aware of. I want him; he wants me. The chemistry between us is out of this world. That doesn't negate any of my reasons for wanting to stay away.

My effort means nothing. I might as well attempt to lift an SUV. The only way he's moving is if he wants to.

Suddenly, he picks me up, kicks open the closest room, and strolls in.

"What are you doing?" He doesn't see fit to answer me, but he throws me on top of the teacher's desk and settles between my legs. "We're in Mr. Green's class! You can't—"

"Watch me." He sweeps the content of the desk aside —pens, a stapler, notes, a pile of manuals—and bends us until my back hits the hard wood.

"Jace!" I protest. "Don't do this."

"Keep going." He licks his lower lip. "It won't make a difference, but I love hearing you beg."

If it were anyone else, I might have thought he was kidding, pushing boundaries for kicks. He'd kiss me, laugh, and we'd be on our way back to PE. But it's Jason Alden. I'm unsurprised to see him open his zipper. "We're at school, dammit! You can't get away with that sort of shit here."

"Just another thing you're wrong about, pretty doll."

"I'll scream," I warn.

"I certainly do hope so."

CHAPTER TWENTY

I kick my legs out, and Jason chuckles, delighted with my protest, holding me firmly under his weight. "Jason, I can't afford to get fucking expelled. Stop this nonsense."

"How many times do I have to tell you I'll take care of you until you believe me, doll?"

I'm about to point out that given our current predicament, I'm entitled to very much doubt that, when a door swings open behind us. Not the one we'd just walked through—the one leading in and out of the teacher's office.

Mr. Green strolls in, professional as usual in his brown blazer over a moss-green sweater.

I expect him to lose it, to yell and send us on our way to the headmaster. Instead, he runs his hand through his sandy hair and sighs. "Jason, this is my classroom. You know I don't mix club business with school."

"What the hell," I say, though I do understand. He said *club business*.

I temporarily lose my will to fight, too flabbergasted, and Jason takes the opportunity to undo the first buttons of my shirt. I whack his hand away and sit up. "Is *anyone* here not part of your kinky group of freaks?"

Mr. Green shrugs. "All employees work for the Heritage, but only two or three of us are members." He fixes Jason with a stern look. "I have one free period now. Be done before the bell." On that note, he makes for the door. "And clean up after yourself," he adds as an afterthought.

Then he's gone, leaving me at Jason's mercy.

He was there the whole time. I'm sure he heard me protest from his office, and he didn't even blink.

"Jason..."

"Nadia," he whispers against my skin, his mouth just inches away. He kisses the side of my neck, and runs his tongue down, until he reaches the spot between my breasts where my shirt's still closed.

Then he takes the fabric either side and tears it open. "Hey! You can't do that. What am I going to wear? Jason, you motherfucker, stop right now!"

His hands reach out for my wrists. He holds my arms up over my head, and transfers one of my wrists to pin them down with one of his. "I think it's time for a reminder, my gorgeous, stubborn doll." His hand moves under my skirt, to the edge of my tights. He yanks them down roughly. "I am in charge."

Fuck!

I writhe, attempting to free my hands, or move my legs, or sit up, but his entire body is primed to keep mine in check. "You're not in charge of my life, asshole. You're not omnipotent."

"No? Then stop me." The next moment, his hot hardness presses at my entrance and slams inside me in one harsh push.

I yelp.

To my chagrin, I was soaked, so his entrance was smooth and painless, but still unexpected. He fills me up so much, I don't think I can even move.

"That's it, doll." His thumb runs over my clit, and I hate the moan that comes out of my throat. "Things are so much better when you let me be in charge."

I didn't let him do anything, he took control. He strips away my free will, until I have no choice but to give in. To let go. And I do.

"This is going to be fast, doll. We wouldn't want to be late for PE, now would we?"

Raw lust and need slam into me, twisting my insides. I stop my useless thrashing. I'm done attempting to tell him what to do. Because I want him to keep going. I want him to fuck me right here, though the door is unlocked and anyone could walk in. Probably *because* of that.

Jason obliges my unspoken request, hips slamming into me again and again. The desk squeaks in protest under me, inching away from the onslaught. "Fucking hell, doll. You're drenched."

I really am.

His hands are on my breasts, one moment caressing them softly, the next, squeezing, pinching. Then his mouth wraps around my nipple and he runs his maddening tongue around the lobe.

"Aahh!" He's pumping in and out of me faster, and harder, and my body jerks as I edge closer and closer to release. I need more. "*Please*."

"You want to come, Nadia?"

I nod eagerly.

"You want me to make you come when you keep saying we don't belong together, that you're fine without me?" He chuckles, punishing me with three deep, punitive thrusts. "I don't think so."

He straightens his spine, withdraws his cock out from me, and as I stare openmouthed, puts his hand on his cock and jerks it hard, once, twice, then a third time. He comes all over my exposed stomach with a grunt.

I stare, frozen in shock, then I start screaming. "Oh, you fucking didn't, you piece of shit!"

"I did." He winks, pulling his trousers up. "You didn't."

"Grrrr!" I stand, indifferent to the fact that I'm mostly naked. "You're never touching me again. Ever!"

"You should at least attempt not to talk nonsense. I'd pay more attention to what you say if you don't, you know."

I want to slap him.

"My pretty doll doesn't like when she's denied orgasms, now does she?"

"Go the fuck away," I seethe.

I'm pulling my tights up, only to find the fucking dick tore them midthighs. I snarl some more. My shirt is toast, so I tie it at the waist and shut my blazer.

Instead of leaving, Jason closes in on me, wrapping his arms around me from the back. "Well, I don't like being ignored. I don't like you pretending to be indifferent to us. Oh, I know you're lying, doll. To me, to yourself. I still fucking hate it. And it's high time you're punished for it."

"Who the fuck do you think you are?"

He kisses the side of my face. "Yours."

CHAPTER TWENTY-ONE

I give up.

When Jason comes to my room after football, I let him. I'm doing my homework, and he joins me for a time, before the touching and the kisses start. Then he makes up for not letting me come at lunch. Three times. We head out to dinner together with the guys. It's nice. More than nice. But I feel so many eyes on me, and I start to grow paranoid. Oh, they're all looking, but at least one of them wants to do a lot more.

As the days pass, I try to relax a little, although the staring never abates.

At the start of the school year, the school bullied me because of Jason. Now, half of them worship me. The other half hates my guts.

On Valentine's Day, I receive an enormous bouquet of two dozen roses at lunch. I roll my eyes at Jason. "What am I going to do with those all day?"

He stares at the flowers like they're a swarm of wasps.

I redirect my attention to the roses and pull out a black card. Other than the florist's logo, there's only one word. *Soon.*

"You didn't send these?" There's a tremble to my voice.

His hand tightens on my shoulder, and he attempts to smile at me, but I see his eyes.

I think I'm going to throw up. That's creepy. Majorly creepy.

I drop the flowers on my tray. "I'm just..."

"Hey, hey. We'll take care of this," he whispers.

The rest of the table is staring at us, but I can't focus on them right now.

"I need to go to the bathroom." I flee.

I know Jason won't like it, but I can't bring myself to care.

In the stall, I stare down at the bowl, feeling bile make its way up my throat. I try to breathe. My heart's racing in my chest, and I feel tears running down my cheeks. I'm not sad; I'm terrified, and just as pissed.

I don't know how long I stay inside, but when I come out of the stall, I notice Brooke, leaning over the sink, up close and personal with the mirror as she touches up her already perfect makeup. Yuki and Sophia stand beside her, the first with her arms crossed, looking bored, and the second, checking her phone.

I'm still shaking, and I hate thinking that those girls could have overheard me as I lost it.

Manon Montgomery and Astrid Nilsson come together. Astrid's a junior, and well on her way to becoming the next Brooke. While she's not my favorite person, we've not really interacted so I don't have much of an opinion.

Brooke shoves her lipstick into her purse and smiles directly at me through the mirror. "Tummy issues?"

"Something like that," I mutter.

She snorts. "I'll bet. I don't blame you. I'd have tried to get a little Alden in me too, in your shoes."

I'm practically shaking with anger I know isn't entirely directed at her. "Well, I didn't. I guess only one of us is a gold-digging slut."

Yuki blows a reluctant laugh she disguises in a cough, while Sophia openly laughs at her sister's expense.

"What the hell?" Brooke demands. "I never did anything to you."

I pause, taken aback, because, well...she has a point.

Brooke did bully Sophia for two years straight, and I was stuck in the middle, but the girl hasn't actually said or done much to me, personally, even when the rest of the school did.

Suddenly I feel ugly and petty too. As Sophia's friend, I've always hated Brooke. I only ever saw her at the enemy, but Sophia dropped me like a hot potato for greener pastures. Maybe I shouldn't take for granted everything she told me, and claim her enemies as my own.

"I'm sorry," I force out. "This isn't about you. I'm

having a shit day." She's right next to me, so I reach out and gently touch her forearm to let her know I mean it. "I know you're not a gold digger, you have plenty of money. And well, you're a slut, but so am I. Sex feels good, right?"

Sophia's gaping in horror, but I tune her out.

As for Brooke, she chokes on a laugh. "Duh."

"Hell, yeah. Especially with Jason," Yuki adds.

Oh, that girl. "Green's definitely your color. He's mine. Get used to it."

I stroll out of there with my head high. I didn't even vomit.

———

Every now and then, our PE class is replaced by outdoor labor disguised as a class, either with the farm, the horses, or gardening. It's meant to teach the spoiled brats of Cross some humility, I think. The jocks are spared, as they need to keep up with their weight and endurance training.

Today, I'm with the horses, although I can't ride. I like horses well enough, and I don't mind mucking their stables as long as I also get to brush them. It's nice, refreshing even, to spend time out of doors, where I get to contemplate just how crazy the campus is.

Much to my surprise, I spy the boys out on the stallions, though they're supposed to be in the gym. Instead, they're playing polo, hooting and hollering, calling out playful insults to one another.

"Typical," Nelly grumbles. "We're cleaning up and they're having fun."

I shrug. We could ride if we knew how.

For the most part, I ignore them, but every so often, I find myself glancing over. More times than not, my gaze lands on Jace. He makes for an impressive sight. He's *so* getting lucky tonight.

Like every night.

"Aren't they supposed to be in endurance class?"

"Ms. Palmer's sick." I glance over my shoulder toward the voice, and see Christoph Billington right in front of the stall I'm cleaning up, and I still.

Good to know, but I prefer remaining ignorant to dealing with him. He took a lot of pleasure in bullying me when Jason gave everyone the green flag to do so. Worse yet, the way he looks at me gives me the creeps.

Chris thinks himself a hotshot, and maybe he is. I don't know him well enough to actually care. I'm not even sure if he knew my name before this year, but he certainly knew the shape of my boobs and ass.

Christoph just stands there, and it's not my job to let him know he's supposed to help out, so I just ignore him. I'm done sweeping and need to mop, so I move past him without saying a word, bend down to grab the water bucket, and return to my stall.

"You have such a nice ass." He licks his lips. I love

when Jason does that, but everything about this guy repulses me. The wet sound, the leer. "I bet you're good at riding."

I don't need a picture to guess what kind of riding he's referring to—the kind that doesn't involve a horse, unless you consider Christoph an animal. Which I do. He'd claim he's a stud.

"Want to go out sometime?" he asks, his smirk growing. "Or stay right here. We can roll around in the hay, since you're so at home in a barn."

Gosh, he's so gross. "Not even in your dreams."

Christoph is a legacy. They don't tend to bother me much, so I'm not sure what his angle is here. Then again, maybe he doesn't have an angle, and is just a creep. I decide he's not worth givings the time of day, and besides, I want to finish up this last stall so I can get to brushing. I've been meaning to sketch some horses lately, and I need to see some up close to study them. I could try to do a kelpie for my next school project.

"Yeah? Well, maybe come to me when Alden dumps your cute, phat ass." He huffs a laugh. "You don't think he's serious about you, do you? Jason has so many pussies at his disposal, you can't even imagine. Nothing special about yours."

I should continue to ignore him instead of feeding the beast, but he's pushed far enough. "Well then, no reason why you should want it. And a good thing, too." I look straight at him. "I'll never want you. You're repulsive, entitled, and quite frankly, not that hot." I bat my lashes.

"Now, this little discussion can stay between us. But one more word, and I spill everything to Jason later. How do you think he'd like you poaching *his* pussy?"

Anyone who knows Jason Alden can answer that question.

As I expected, Christoph huffs and storms off.

I let out a breath and glance out at the field. Jace catches my eye immediately. Oh, he's going to have questions.

Poor Chris.

CHAPTER TWENTY-TWO

"I'm going to kill him."

"You can't murder Chris for being gross. It's like killing a spider just because they're creepy. He can't help it."

"I can and I will," Jace announces cheerfully.

I could point out that murder would lead to jail time, but the truth is, he'd probably just ask his dad to cover it up. So instead, I remind him, "We're already running late. Are we plotting murder or are we going somewhere?"

He, unlike me, is dressed to kill, in black slacks, a buttoned-down ivory shirt open to his chest, and black shoes that look as if they've been polished for hours to a high shine. I imagine him making some poor student do it before class.

I'm wearing nothing but a towel, because he only informed me that I was supposed to get ready for ten minutes ago. "I don't have a fancy dress in my dorm room," I'd reasoned.

Then I remembered that I do, thanks to him.

In my walk-in closet, I look through the number of garments on hangers, flipping through various shades and fabrics. I could swear my collection of dresses and shoes increased in the last month and a half.

"You made this?" he calls from my room.

I glance to find him standing next to my desk. Oh, shit, I forgot to cover the sculpture.

My new desktop's on the floor, to make room for the large sculpture I started in art class a few days ago. We do so many daily projects, we tend to throw out most of them, but I brought this one back with me to finish.

I need to build up as much art as possible for my portfolio in case I get an interview for college.

I hate that he's looking at the bust on my desk. For one, it's unfinished, and I'm always sensitive about people seeing a work-in-progress. When he grins, there's no doubt that he recognizes himself.

Really, I didn't have a choice but to sculpt him. Everything about him is so damn sexy, all lines and angles that make him the perfect subject. "If you break that bust, I am going to go ape-shit on you," I warn.

"Break it? I'm going to steal it and put it on our mantelpiece at home."

My cheeks flush. Lifting my chin, I smirk at him. "I plan on setting it on fire," I claim. "Therapeutic, don't you think?"

"And appropriate." He nods. "Get dressed. We're going to be late."

I scoff and shake my head. "Yeah, well maybe we wouldn't be late if you'd told me I was supposed to get ready ahead of time. At least tell me where we're going."

"What's the fun in that?" He's cocky as ever.

"It's Thursday. Can't it wait until tomorrow?" The winter break is starting this week.

"No, it can't, I'm afraid. After all, there's only one Black and White opening."

My jaw drops.

I follow art news, especially local news, so I'm aware that a co-op of seriously talented, upscale artists are opening their own gallery. It's a private venue, strictly invite-only, but they've set up one public day per month. I'd totally planned to visit as soon as I could. But to be there at the opening? Meet the owners, investors, the artists?

"Oh shit." I pick up the first dress I get my hands on. They're all gorgeous anyway.

He meanders over to my bed, his hands splayed behind him to support himself as he watches me drop my towel and drag red velvet along my limbs. "Aren't I the best boyfriend?"

"Are you?" I challenge. "You still haven't asked me out. And I haven't accepted."

"I'm not one for rhetorical questions."

The mermaid gown hugs all my curves in the right places. Loving what I see in my full-length mirror, I select two pairs of shoes, following my mother's advice this time: I'll wear the flats and put heels on at the last minute.

"I love that color on you."

"You chose it. And everyone looks good in red."

"Agree to disagree."

I hurry to the bathroom and start on my makeup, my excitement making me clumsier than usual. I decide to pass on the liner, rather than risk messing it up.

When I return, Jace is flipping through the pages of my sketchbook. Part of me wants to rip my art from his hands. It's a lot more personal than checking out my panty drawer, and of course, the arrogant ass did so without even asking for permission.

But the thing is, I don't actually mind him looking at it, somehow.

He shuts it and gives me a slow once-over, his gaze lifting from my ballerina flats up my legs, taking his sweet time before he reaches my eyes. "I changed my mind. We're staying right here." Gaze hooded, he looks like he's considering devouring my mouth.

"I don't think so," I say, though minutes ago, I was the one arguing to stay on campus. "I'm not missing the opening."

David's waiting for us when we get in front of the lake. It's been six weeks and I'm still just as red-faced every time I look at his pretty blue eyes.

He's a professional and has never so much as sent me

an inappropriate look, but I'm not about to forget what he's seen. The way he looked at me.

Car rides are always filled with an equal dose of tension, apprehension, and dare I say, anticipation. And that's just for the three minutes it takes us to reach the U from the lake. This time, he's driving us into town.

Almost as soon as the door shuts behind us, Jason pulls me into his lap, completely indifferent to traffic regulations.

"Don't you dare mess with my makeup," I tell him.

I want to make a good impression in front of whoever we meet tonight, and looking all mussed after an hour of messing around in the back of a car has never impressed anybody.

But instead he just kisses my exposed shoulder and asks me what artist I'm most looking forward to meeting today.

CHAPTER TWENTY-THREE

David drops us off in front of an honest-to-god red carpet leading up to the lower Manhattan gallery currently surrounded by paparazzi.

Even the architecture is stunning, a work of art in and of itself, and I can't wait to get inside. There's a bit of a line, though, and cameras flash.

One of the paps spots Jace before we're off the curb, and I blink at the flashes of cameras. He wraps his arm around my waist and leads us up to the gallery.

"Jason, Jason, who are you wearing?"

"Jason, boxers or briefs?"

"Jason, who is that with you today, a special lady?"

We've almost reached the end of the line when Jace turns to answer that last question with a dazzling smile. "Very special." He kisses the top of my head and on that note, we head out of the cold and into a beautiful white hall filled with fashionable, trendy people.

"That was insane. You're just a high school guy, not some celebrity."

"Why can't I be both?" He offers me his elbow and I take it. "This way."

A smiling server offers us champagne, visibly unconcerned about our age. I'm no stranger to wine but I've actually never tried champagne. It's delicious.

My mouth drops as I take in the first piece of art on display, a smooth, larger-than-life pair of lovers carved in black stone. "My god!"

"Titans, actually. Not gods." A young, olive-skinned man in a purple winks. "Sylvan Doyles, at your service."

"You made this," I gush, as I spotted the name carved at the feet of the gargantuan shapes. "It's incredible. Like, how?"

"With scaffolding, a saw, a lot of time, and too much money." He winks. "I doubt I'll make it back; pieces like these rarely ever sell. I do smaller stuff too, though. Garden statues, fountain pieces, the like. But my Greek series, it comes from the heart, you know?"

"I can tell." My heart is racing. It's the first art piece I see, the first artist I talk to, and I've never been so elated in my life.

"So, which Titans are those?"

"Uranus and Gaia, obviously." Sylvan throws his hands in the air in frustration. It's obvious he's tired of answering that question. "Who else would I start with?"

Who, indeed.

SPIN THE DAMN BOTTLE

"I can't wait to see more." I could stay and chat forever, but there's too much for me to discover.

We keep strolling through the gallery, though extremely slowly, as I keep stopping to gape and exclaim and occasionally shout.

One piece renders me utterly silent, though I can't express why. It's an abstract with violent strokes of red and black, yet it brings forth so much emotion.

"What do you see?" Jace wonders.

"I don't know, a flower in the rain? Or maybe a howling lone wolf. It's not about what I see, it's about how I feel."

"Now, this lady has an eye." A man with an easy smile and a crisp suit joins us, his hand patting the back of Jason's jacket. "And a heart, which is more important. You should keep her close."

"I intend to. Harold, this is my Nadia. Nadia, Harold Hurst, art collector and one of my grandfather's close friends."

I shake his hand politely. "A pleasure."

"My, isn't she delightful?" He returns to the painting. "He has great talent, that boy. Luther Marks. He came to us wanting to draw comics. Five years later, he's doing it for one of the best publications in the country *and* he paints in his spare time."

"Harold is on the board at Tisch."

My jaw drops.

Of course he is.

And of course Jason would introduce us. If I know

him well, and I do, this is the very reason we're here in the first place.

Holy fuck.

"Woah. That's...woah."

"Now, my boy Jason let me know you're interested in attending our school, and that makes you a discerning young lady. I told him that we'd look at your file. No guarantees, mind you. We recruit on merit alone. But I'm so glad you've chosen us, Ms. Reyes. So glad."

He follows us for the next two paintings. Knowledgeable and easy to talk to, he's good company, though my nerves are all over the place. Unless I'm very much mistaken, this is more important than nailing my interview with the admissions department.

When he makes his excuses to go chat with another group, he congratulates Jason on choosing "such a delightful soul," and to me, says, "We'll be in touch."

I watch him leave, whispering, "I don't know if I want to kiss you or throttle you for not giving me a warning!"

"I figured you didn't need the stress." Jason's entirely remorseless.

"I had champagne!"

"And it relaxed you." He wraps his arms around me and holds me close. "You did great. He loved you."

"He would have loved a harpy, so long as she was attached to your arm," I mutter.

Jason huffs in amusement. "Hardly. Old Harold is a hardass. He takes art seriously. He meant what he said:

he'll look at your file, and only accept you after he realizes you are incredibly talented."

Hopefully that's true, but I'll never know whether I deserve my place now.

We're almost at the end of the gallery when a man waves at Jason. Fashionable and less exuberant than is the norm here, he approaches with purposeful steps.

"Carlos!" Jace takes the man's hand.

"Is this the girl?"

"It is indeed. Nadia, Carlos is one of the artists and owners of Black and White. He's the one we owe tonight's invitation to."

"Thank you so much," I say, eagerly shaking his palm. "I'm having a great time."

"Oh, anytime, darling. Listen, Jason tells me you don't display anything yet, right?" He speaks fast, and doesn't give me enough time to try and answer. "We sold more than I'd planned today, so I have the space for a small series—three to five pieces, something like that. If that works, we can build from there."

I stare in complete disbelief.

"I sent him the bust and a few of your sketches," Jason tells me, like it's an explanation. It isn't.

High school kids don't get to be displayed in up-and-coming galleries. They just don't.

"I, I..." I clear my throat. "A series," I repeat. "Sculptures, right? Busts?"

"I'm keeping most of the art for a month then I have

to send it to the buyers. Can you manage three to five by then?"

I fumble to agree, barely managing to get a "yes" out.

"Grand. If you'll excuse me." Carlos touches Jace's arm and turns to me. "It was very nice to meet you."

"Yeah, nice," I echo.

"Keep me updated in two weeks, yeah?"

I nod and he flees toward other guests.

I watch him retreat, my excitement tempered with a fair dose of shame.

I would never have been here without Jason. Carlos wouldn't have bothered to look at any of my finished art, let alone rough sketches.

This world is about who you know. Having talent isn't enough.

I know one thing, though.

Jason Alden did all of this for no other reason than to please me.

He's full of contradictions, chief among them his tendency to completely ignore my desires and, moments later, worship me like a queen. A relationship with him is a constant rollercoaster of emotions, but like a little kid just done with a terrifying ride, I can't help but jump right back in line for another turn.

CHAPTER TWENTY-FOUR

Not every piece of art is as enticing as Sylvan Doyles' by a long shot. Some are quite soulless, verging on boring.

Knowing that Carlos was happy to display mine after a quick glance at sketches through a text, simply because Jason Alden had sent the message, I'm not surprised. When you value the *who* more than the *what*, you're bound to end up with some lackluster products.

We eventually finish our tour, and Jace has plenty of trendy, fashionable buyers and well-known names in the industry to introduce to me, but by the time I start to grow bored, he leans in close, his breath hot on my skin. "Do you want to get out of here?"

"Let's."

We schmooze some more on our way out, but within less than half an hour, we're back on the cold New York streets. There are far fewer members of the press gathered outside now, but the dozen left are as fascinated with Jason as before. If I was under any delusion that he's someone normal, they'd have stripped me of them.

David comes to save us in the burgundy town car, appearing mere seconds after we come out of the new gallery. By the time we've made our way back through the red carpet, he's opened the passenger door, and we slide inside.

"This beats public transport," I admit. "Though I can't imagine how much you pay him for a job that mostly consists of driving ten minutes per day."

I'll never understand the elite.

"It doesn't matter how much we pay him," Jason says, haughty as ever.

I can't believe this guy. He must realize how ridiculous he sounds, sometimes. "Do you have golden toilet in your private jet? I feel like you would."

"So judgmental." Jason lifts my knuckles to his lips and kisses them. "I didn't use to have a driver. Rowan has one, and that's enough for the four of us. David used to work security for my father, and got hurt in the line of duty. We offered a generous package but he didn't want to retire, so Dad sent him to me. A job standing all day and following him around wasn't suitable anymore. It doesn't matter how much we're paying him because the point is taking care of a loyal employee."

I eye him suspiciously. "Did you just make that up to make me feel bad?"

His smile shows all of his white teeth, and his steel

eyes flash with something playfully wicked. "You think so little of me? Tut, tut. What will you give me if I'm telling the truth?"

By his tone alone, I'm one hundred percent certain every word was a fact. Jason isn't the sort to make bets he might lose. Still, I want to play. "I'm game."

He pretends to think it through. "If I didn't mislead you, you'll come to play with me at Midnight. If I did... hm." He tilts his head. "What could you possibly want from me?"

Nothing I'm not already getting. Instead of searching for a desire he's not already fulfilling, I choose something I know will drive him insane. "You let me take control. I'll bind your hands behind your back and do whatever I want to you."

I actually love the way he leads us in bed, but relinquishing control isn't something a guy like him can easily do.

Not that it matters. I'm going to lose. And I don't mind one bit.

Jason knocks once at the partition separating us from the driver.

"Sir?"

"Nadia was curious how you came to work for my spoiled ass, David."

He looked at me in the rearview mirror. "Mr. Alden senior was in a bit of a bind a while back. I got knifed in the knee protecting him, so I can't work security like I used to. I'm glad for the new assignment, though. Jason certainly has interesting car rides."

That's as close to talking about my little peep show as he's ever gotten. I blush furiously.

"Satisfied?" Jason's smug as ever.

"Not yet."

————

I didn't expect us to head to Midnight Elites *right then*. After the night I've had, returning to my luxurious bed sounds like a great idea.

"We have school tomorrow," I point out when David stops at the entrance of the club.

"It's the last day before the winter break. Do you really think anyone's going to care if we're hungover?"

"No one would care year-round for you," I grumble. I doubt any teacher would ever dare to give him anything worse than a B minus, even if he submitted a blank paper.

Me, not so much.

"Come on, doll. Live a little." He winks and walks out of the car, one hundred percent certain I'll follow.

Smug ass.

I switch my ballerina flats for my heels again before following him. The moment we walk inside the dark, sensual hall, I forget all tiredness.

The music is as seductive as I remember, and I'm drawn to the packed dance floor like moth to a flame. It might be a weeknight, but that doesn't deter the center of well-dressed, beautiful young men and women here. Clearly, Midnight Elites isn't hurting for customers.

Jason joins me, and I grin as we sway to the rhythm of the drums. Damn, the man can move. We whirl together, his body so fucking perfect against mine, and his light touch over my red gown increasing my hunger for more.

"Drink?" His gaze dips to my painted lips. "You look rather thirsty."

I bob my head up and down at least three times. "I'm parched."

I'm not surprised he takes me up the flight of stairs instead of simply heading to the closest bar. He knows my thirst isn't the kind any liquid can quench.

The sound of the music is dimmer upstairs, and the lighting, slightly brighter. The decor has changed since the last time I was here, in November. Instead of dark leather upholstery, the booths are white and pink, and the neons are cool blue rather than warm yellows.

The design might have changed, but the vibe? Not so much. The most different thing in this room is me. Instead of averting my eyes, I look. I look everywhere. I watch strangers blow, jerk off, and fuck each other in every hole.

My time with Jason has made me a different person. Part of me realizes that if this thing between us ends, I'll likely struggle to fit into what used to be the norm to me. Our society considers sex the nastiest possible sin and hides it at all costs, hence why they're just fine showing violence, lies, and thievery to children only a few years old, but movies with so much as a mention of sexual awareness are banned for anyone under fifteen. Plus, that notion that monogamy is the only possible way a relationship should function is getting more and more bizarre to me. I'm with Jason, and no one else, but we both enjoy bringing a third party into our games, and I fail to see what's wrong with that. I'd hate to *cheat* upon agreed rules of engagement, but playing the game together is another story entirely.

I don't think I could be with a man who'd demand to be the only thing I see, the only person I'm allowed to act on my attraction with. Not when I've had a taste of the other side.

"This way." Jason takes my hand and leads me out of the main area, to a side room that's closed but unlocked.

Inside, the room's set up like a smaller and comfortable lounge. The two large, deep green, velvet chesterfield sofas are pushed against opposite walls, and the coffee table was omitted to leave an open area at the center.

"Hey!" A silver-blonde beauty with the most adorable polka dot sundress grins up at Jason.

I stare in disbelief, because that's most definitely Sarah Dee Frank, the *Sweet Farm of Mine* child actress who moved on to become America's sweetheart, taking on role after role where she's basically playing the same adorable, innocent ingenue who get rescued by a hot dude.

"Sarah Dee."

She sends an air kiss to Jason as I come to terms with

the reality that I'm standing in front of a girl I used to worship when I was seven, only to notice the four members of Transcendence, including their crazy hot lead singer Harry Voss, with his sexy black hair and his dark, kohl-lined eyes. Then I see Paul Reich—solo guitarist—and Nanee Laumer, who just started an incredible line of shoes. If someone had asked me for the top ten most successful young people of our time, all seven present would have made the cut.

They're huddled on the floor like wayward children. I half expect to see that they're playing with marbles, but when we approach, I notice a bottle on the floor.

"Who's the pretty lady?" Harry fucking Voss asks, presumably referring to me, given that he's staring my way.

He said I was pretty, and if I were the dramatic sort, I could faint.

"This is my Nadia." He tugs me closer.

"Nadia!" Sarah Dee beams. "*Love* the dress. I bet you're the reason we haven't seen much of this boy around for a while."

Jason shrugs and answers for me. "She's new to the club, and I don't play without her. She owes me a game, though. What's the poison tonight?"

"Seven minutes in heaven." Nanee reaches for the glass cola bottle in front of her and twists it between her middle finger and her thumb until it moves in rapid circles.

The motion slows and finally stops, pointing to Harry.

"No, no, no, that *doesn't* count." The Transcendence bass player, Jeremy Hault, glares at Nanee. "Jace and Nad weren't seated yet. Plus, it's fucking boring, as you two are together anyway."

They are?

I glance between the hot-ass singer and the petite, warm honey-skinned beauty. "God, you're going to make pretty babies." My words spill out before I can help it, and the entire group chuckles.

"Neither of us has time for that, but we totally would," Nanee concurs.

Jason lowers himself to sit between Jeremy and the drummer, Oscar, who shifts to make enough room for me. "Thank you. So, what are the rules?"

"What, you've never played spin the bottle?" Sarah Dee dramatically widens her eyes. "Were you completely neglected as a child? Blink twice if you need help."

"I'm just guessing your rules are a little different than the ones we followed in third grade."

"Not really, no." Nanee giggles. "You spin the damn bottle, you get seven minutes in heaven with whoever it's pointing to."

"Just not in the closet," Harry says, winking at me. "We like to watch."

Jesus. My lips are suddenly so very dry, and I have to run my tongue over them. "All right. Sounds like fun."

A hell of a lot of fun.

CHAPTER TWENTY-FIVE

anee gets a second turn, and this time the bottle points to Sarah Dee. I gape and most of the guys clap. Jeremy pumps his fist in the air in a universal sign of victory.

The two women are no less enthused.

"Right, you know the rules. Seven minutes. If one of you comes, one point, if both of you come, three points. And absolutely *no* faking." Harry is all business. "We'll set the points back to zero, since we have newcomers."

"What? That's not fair!" Nick, Oscar's twin, and the second guitarist and violist of Transcendence, has a serious pout. "You're only saying that because you were losing!"

"We'd only played three rounds." Sarah Dee rolls her eyes at him. "Unless you don't think you can come again, old man."

He shoots her the finger.

"All right, timer's ready when you are." Harry has a finger on his watch, waiting for a signal.

"You wanna drive or ride, gorgeous?" Nanee asks the actress.

"It's your spin. You're the one in charge."

Nanee grins, and crawls across the floor to the blonde.

"No touching before the timer starts." Harry's seriously invested in following the rules of engagement.

"Ready when you are, darling," she tells her boyfriend, though her attention's entirely on Sarah Dee.

"And...go."

Nanee wastes no time, spreading Sarah Dee's long legs and burying her head between her pink summer dress. The actress throws her head back and moans, arching her spine. She gathers her skirt past her waist, baring her milky thighs. She's not wearing anything other than thigh-high socks. Her pelvic hair's trimmed in a tiny, neat heart.

I cross my legs, feeling my core heat and tighten.

"Holy fuck, Nan," Sarah moans. "You're so good with your tongue."

"Isn't she just," Harry says, his voice rough.

Of their own volition, the inner muscles of my thighs contract and let go. I'm loving the friction, so I keep going.

Nanee's relentless, her head moving in every direction, tongue out. She licks. She blows. She rubs with her fingertips and curls digits right inside Sarah Dee's cunt, fucking her fast and hard.

"That's it. Right there, Nan. Please keep going. Yes, yes, yes!" Sarah screams.

I watch her convulse, her entire body trembling before she goes limp. Nanee looks up between her legs and winks at her, before glancing at her boyfriend. "Time?"

"Two minutes, twenty seconds left."

"Got it." She tries to shimmy out of her leather pants as fast as she can, but it still takes her a good long while. Underneath, she's in a lacy black thong that she removes a lot faster.

Sarah Dee hooks her right leg over Nanee's and hops forward, until the apex of their thighs meet. They both start to move together, breathing hard and fast.

"One minute," Harry announces, driving them to move faster.

Nanee leans forward and kisses Sarah Dee's mouth, as they keep scissoring each other.

"Jesus," I whisper, as my heart races in my chest.

I wouldn't have even thought I was much into girls until now, but oh my god, this is fucking hot.

"You like to watch, too, hm?" Jason whispers, running his tongue along my neck.

Definitely.

"And, time! Good effort, girls, but only one point."

"Feels like at least a hundred," Sarah Dee purrs, still

rubbing against the other woman's pussy, though she moves slower.

"Now, girls, you know the rules." Who would have known a rock legend was so into following rules? "And we need room for the next spin. Move. You can get back to that after the game."

Nanee sighs, but she does stop fucking her friend, gathers her things and gets back to her place—though she doesn't bother to pull the trousers or panties back on.

"Who spins now?" I ask Jason, but I must have spoken louder than I thought.

"It's Nanee's choice," Jeremy tells me. "And Nanee always picks Harry."

"*Always*." Oscar rolls his eyes at her.

"Nadia can have the next go." She sticks her tongue out at him. "That'll show you."

I stare at her in horror. Shit. I have to do this. Next. It's my turn.

Over the last few weeks, I've accepted a lot of things about myself, what I like, what I want to try. I want this. I'm still so freaking nervous when I have to take charge, though.

I glance at Jason, and he holds my stare, unreadable. I don't doubt he'll get me out of here if I want him to. Not for one second.

I get to my knees and lean over to take the bottle. In one look, I sweep over the entire room. After I spin, I'm going to touch one of them. Harry, Jeremy, Oscar, Nick, and Paul are every straight girl's fantasy throughout the country. I wouldn't have thought Sarah Dee and Nanee were my type about eight minutes ago. Now, I'm not so sure.

I stare down at the bottle.

Then I spin.

CHAPTER TWENTY-SIX

The glass bottle pirouettes across the cold stone floor.

I sit back on my heels and watch it turn for a lot longer than it did for Nanee. At least, it feels like it. It starts to slow down, and I glance up to the direction of the neck. Nick. Paul. Nanee... For a second, I think it might stop at the beautiful Indian girl, but the bottle keeps going until it's pointing right at her boyfriend.

I stare up at Harry Voss, astounded. I think my stomach drops, but it's certainly not in disappointment. Apprehension, maybe. Anticipation, certainly.

"Someone else is going to have to time." He removes his watch and dangles it in the air, indifferent to who picks it up. His eyes are staying focused on me. "You ready for me, pretty lady?"

I swallow the clog in my throat, but I nod. Then I immediately glance at Jason. He only smirks and lies back, hands flat behind him, everything about his posture expressing he's just fine with this development.

Harry Voss stands and crosses the circle to reach me. "Are we trying for a one or a three?"

I'm confused, uncertain about what those options entail. "A three is we both orgasm, right? Is that even possible in seven minutes?"

Everyone chuckles.

"It's ambitious, I'll admit," Harry concedes, sitting between Jason and I. "But after that display, I'm hard as fuck so I'll come fast. How about you, Nadia?"

I'm soaked and my insides are so fucking tight. I could have come just by rubbing my thighs, really. And this is Harry Voss. "Yeah. I think...yeah."

"A three it is." He looks over at his bandmate, armed with his watch. "Ready?"

"I'll call it on three. Two. One..." Oscar makes this number last. "Show time."

Harry's hand hooks around the back of my neck, and his dark eyes bore into me before his hot mouth closes over mine. Fuck. I'm kissing Harry Voss. Really kissing him, deep and hard, like I'm starved for more. His free hand runs along my thighs, burning everywhere it touches.

I bend toward him, and he lets me tower over him, leaning back.

He lets go of both my leg and neck to fiddle with the opening of his slacks. As he strives to free his hard length, I get rid of my tights, and slide the length of my dress up. By the time I'm done, I can feel a hot, velvet-soft member right on my inner leg. I don't let go of his mouth, as I take it in my fist, and direct it at my entrance.

My eyes rise to look at Jason as I lower myself on Harry's cock, slowly, feeling every inch in that position.

"Four minutes," Oscar offers unprompted.

Almost half of our time is gone.

Harry thrusts up, hard, slamming inside me. "Oh, god."

He hisses as he lowers his hips, and pushes inside me again. He's thicker than what I'm used to, and fills me to the brink.

His large hands find my waist, anchoring me. I place my palms on his chest and squat over him. Then I lower my weight on his cock. He grunts, throwing his head back. "Fucking hell, Nadia, you're so fucking hot."

I ride him hard and fast, taking my pleasure. He thrusts up to meet me, slapping against my ass again and again, and again.

Harry's hand moves from my waist to my breasts, and roughly pushes the hem of my dress down, uncovering my bra. He shoves his hand underneath and palms one, softly at first, then rough.

I start to pant as my insides tighten.

"Fuck, fuck, fuck. You're getting so tight. *Fuck.* I'm gonna come inside you, Nadia."

Thank fuck I actually did get on contraception. Does anyone use condom here? I should have asked, at least.

"You'd better be clean, asshole," I manage between grunts.

He chuckles, sitting up to push my bra out of the way and wrap his mouth over my nipple. His hand finds my clit, and start to rub.

I lose it.

"Ahh. Ahh. Ahh..."

"One minute left."

My vision catches Jason over Harry's dark hair. He's pulled his cock out and started to touch himself, slowly, eyes straight on me.

"That's it, gorgeous, come for me."

I do. I explode around him with a long wail, and he keeps fucking me through it, prolonging the rapture. With a final hard thrust and a broken grunt, Harry reaches his release, and goes limp under me.

We both huff and pant.

"Holy shit, man. That's a three."

Nanee claps excitedly. "That was hot as fuck."

"You don't say." Jason brings his hand to my face and strokes my cheek.

Only then do I think to move, and hop on his lap.

Jason kisses the top of my head and hugs me hard, knowing exactly what I need.

"Who's next, doll?"

CHAPTER TWENTY-SEVEN

We don't even consider heading back to Cross.

We play for almost three hours, at least twenty rounds of the game. Everyone gets about three turns.

Never have I strived so hard to win a game. When the bottle pointed at me on Paul's turn, I threw my head back and let him lick me until I screamed. He jerked off, and we earned another three. On Jason's turn, I watched him take Sarah Dee from behind, and I was startled by the way I felt. So fucking horny. Proud that this stunning, sexy man is mine. There isn't room for a shadow of jealousy. How could there be, when I know he wants *me?*

"How do you feel?" Jason asks on the way to his parents' place in NoHo.

"Sticky."

He snorts, pulling me closer. "I'll bet."

"I can't believe you let Jeremy blow you."

That makes him chuckle. "You were gasping the whole time. I don't know why you're surprised, though. Jeremy has a mouth and knows what to do with it." He's relaxed as ever, and I feel a little foolish, because indeed, why wouldn't he be? I was just fine letting Sarah Dee finger me on my last round. "If it's a wet hole, I don't mind fucking it."

"So, we're bisexual," I muse in amazement.

"Pansexual, in my case. Women are easier, as society is still about two centuries out of pace with human nature. We can thank the modern organized religions for that." The car stops in front of a brownstone not unlike my parents' in Brooklyn, albeit a little larger. Except, in this neighborhood, the place must be worth ten million at least. "We're home."

As we head out, I'm somewhat taken aback by the normalcy of the building. "I was expecting something, I don't know, flashier."

The Aldens are one of the richest families in the world. While the house, and its location, are certainly impressive in and of themselves, they don't scream multi-billionaire.

"Flashy doesn't go with my father's image. He's a left-wing senator, remember? A man of and for the people."

I giggle as he guides me to the threshold.

Inside, the place epitomizes sophistication. High walls, floor-to-ceiling windows fitted with pale drapes that fall to the floor like dresses. Three walls are cream, the fourth, naked red brick. I could stand in the entryway's fireplace. "Yeah. The people definitely have halls like these."

"Smartass." He walks up a grand staircase, bypassing the first floor. Upstairs, we cross white double doors and reach a modern self-sufficient apartment.

The open-plan kitchen and lounge are black and white, and at the very center of the room, there's a gleaming grand piano. "You play?"

Jason wrinkles his nose. "Not anymore. We've redecorated the floor several times, but my mother always 'forgets' to have the piano moved out." He rolls his eyes. "She just wants to show off her boy's music at parties again."

"Why don't you call a removal service?" The look he sends me would have made me shiver a while back. Now, I smirk. "Who would have thought? Jason Alden, a momma's boy."

"Yeah, well, she lost one of her boys. I'm not about to upset her over a stupid piano."

That's sobering. "It's sweet that you think about her. It'd probably be sweeter if you played for her, though."

"I think not. This way."

His bedroom here is smaller than mine at Cross, though the bed's certainly large enough for a party of five. Just looking at it, I realize I'm dead on my feet.

"Shower first, Ms. Sticky."

I pout. "Do I have to?"

Jason wraps one of his arms around my back and the second behind my knees, and carries me into his en suite.

His slate-tiled shower is huge, with a built-in bench and two double shower heads. He sets me down on the bench and starts the shower, checking the temperature. "All right, doll." He drags the hand shower to me and start hosing me down with the strong jets. The warmth feels delicious against my skin.

"You spoil me."

"I intend to keep doing so." He hooks the shower back on its stand and lathers my skin with a fragrant soap. "You were incredible today, jumping right into the fray. I expected you to take more of an observational role your first time playing."

"I loved it." I bite my lower lip. "I loved watching you, too. With Sarah Dee, with Jeremy." I chuckle. "I especially loved winning."

"It's not exactly fair. I only had two turns, and the fucking bottle never pointed to me."

He stands to retrieve the showerhead, and seated as I am, his crotch is right at eye level. His cock's soft, though still quite large. "Poor Jason, all neglected." My gaze finds his eyes and I keep it there as my hand takes him in my fist.

"I thought you were tired," he reminds me.

"Never too tired for that." He's already hard, even before I wrap my lips around the head of his cock.

I barely touched him today, and after all that, I want to feel him. And I do.

I move my head up and down his shaft, slow, taking him as deep as I can.

"Fuck, doll. You're so good with that mouth." He takes a handful of my hair, inherently incapable of relinquishing control.

I let him. He controls my rhythm, making me take him faster, then slower.

"My balls," he grits between his teeth.

I grasp them in my hand and start massaging them, unsure what feels good.

"Yeah, that's it. Oh, fuck." He abruptly withdraws from my mouth and tugs my hair upward. I get to my feet, and he turns me around. My hands flat on the bench, I lift my hips a little higher.

His hardness presses at my entrance, but only teases my folds, rubbing along the drenched opening. Then he moves it higher than expected, against my asshole. "Has anyone touched you there before?"

I shake my head, and he moves his cock back to my pussy. I gasp a needy moan when he rams it inside.

"I'll take you there soon." A finger teases my other hole as he moves in and out of my pussy, curving inside. "How would you like that?"

The unexpected pressure feels good. More than good. "I don't know."

"I do. You're gonna fucking love it." His cock batters my sensitive walls so quickly. "You know why? Because you're mine."

"Yours," I repeat in agreement, collapsing forward.

My knees are shaking, barely even supporting me. He tugs my hair back and barrels deeper, faster. I've been fucked so much tonight, the friction is painful, but the fire raging inside me needs a release. I push back against his hips as he slams home.

Then, we finally crash.

CHAPTER TWENTY-EIGHT

J ason cooks. Who would have guessed? Certainly not I.

We wake up earlier than we might have, considering the fact that we didn't get to bed until three in the morning, and Jason makes us an omelet and crispy bacon. I'm seriously starving, and no wonder, given last night's events.

"Marry me," I tease after the first perfect mouthful.

"We have class today. Tomorrow, if you want."

"Class?" I make a face.

It's already eight; our first lesson will start in a moment.

"It's the last day before break and I need some stuff from my room for the holiday. Might as well go to class. I mean, you might not need to, given your likely acceptance into Tisch, but some of us haven't heard from our colleges of choice yet."

The events of the previous night rush back to me. In light of all the delicious depravity, I'd practically forgotten the Black and White opening. "I mean, I might not get in."

"You're incredibly talented. You will."

He doesn't mention the obvious: good old Harold will probably let me in over someone as deserving, simply because of Jason.

After breakfast, David drives us back to Cross and Roses, just in time for us to get changed into our uniforms and head to lit class.

The school is what it always was, bustling and full of spoiled elite kids, but somehow, after last night, I feel different. I feel part of something. When I see a legacy in the corridor, I smile, feeling like we share a secret.

Christoph Billington's face is no less sickening. He catches me on my way to art class and leers. "Hey, Reyes. I hear you were at Alden's club last night." He ogles me from the tip of my toes up to my breasts, never bothering to get to my eyes. "I would have loved to be there for a taste. Let me know next time."

"I'm never going to let you touch me, Chris." I mean it, too.

I might not have personally known any of the players last night, but I liked them, was comfortable with them, or I wouldn't have done what I did. Christoph gives me the creeps. He takes women—or at least, me—for granted. He's probably never had to work for it, so he fails to understand that he needs to be a decent person for women to want him.

Jason might have a long list of vices, and can't exactly qualify as the nicest man in the world, but he's never made me feel like a piece of meat he could buy. Jason is interested in my likes and dislikes, in my dreams and desires, hence why he brought me to the Black and White opening. He might be twisted and have the moral compass of a cat, but to him, I'm a person. Oh, he's spoiled. If he wants something I'm not willing to give, he's likely to coerce me into giving in. Christoph is the kind who just takes.

"Yeah?" He's highly amused. "Even at your debut?"

I frown, not understanding him.

"Oh, he didn't tell you, did he?" He chuckles and takes a step forward.

His stench—tobacco and a strong, heady cologne—assaults my nostrils.

He bends to whisper in my ear, and I want to pull away, but I also refuse to show just how much he gets to me, so I stay put.

"When we let a poor little whore like you into the Heritage, her grand debut starts with her tied up to a swing with her legs wide open, letting all of us juniors do whatever we please to her."

He's joking, right?

"I'm going to take my sweet, sweet time with you, Reyes. I'm going to fuck all of your holes and come all over your tits."

I bring my knee to his crotch, hitting him hard.

"You bitch!" he croaks.

"This is the closest I'll ever get to your dick, asshole. You disgust me," I snarl, before retreating to class, heart galloping.

He was lying, right? Jason would have told me. He would have...

I know exactly what he would have done if that was true. Jason would prepare me for it. Make me touch others, make me crave debased, debauched things. Groom me into the kind of person who wouldn't mind it.

If I'm honest with myself, the picture Christoph painted doesn't shock me. It wouldn't even repulse me if the likes of that repugnant ape wasn't in the picture.

When I get to the art studio, still shaking, I pull my phone out and type a quick text.

Me: **I need to talk to you.**

Jason sends a thumbs-up, nothing more.

Mr. Weir soon enters and makes us get to work.

After class, David's waiting for me as usual, to bring me back to Glass. I pace in my room while Jason and the others are at practice, frustration and anger rising with every passing minute.

He walks through my door without knocking at five thirty. "Hey, doll."

"Is it true your club does some sick initiation ritual?" I glare, challenging and defiant.

Jason, still in his football uniform, raises an eyebrow. "Who told you?"

"Well, is it?" I push.

He shrugs. "In most instances, sure. It's supposed to be secret, though. Who spoke to you about it?"

"Chris," I spit.

"Of course. Chris. He does love the debutantes, that pervert." Jason laughs. "Don't look at me like that. You don't have to go through it. In fact, you don't even have to join the group if you don't want to. It would make things easier for me, but I won't push the issue."

Some of my ire leaves me. "Oh."

"I'm a member, though, and I wouldn't like attending private club events without you." He sheds his shirt, revealing the sculptural torso I'm intimately familiar with. "Christ, Coach is a dick before the breaks. Do you mind if I get in your tub?"

I nod my agreement, making my way to the platform and starting the water. "I don't like Chris," I say. "I wouldn't want to be part of a club that forces me to do things with guys like that."

"I already said you don't. The debutante and male initiate hazing is for petals who become blossoms, or the thorns who turn to stems—the recruits club members bring into our folds to join our ranks. You're not a petal or a blossom. You're *my* woman."

I don't think I understand. "What's the difference?"

"They have something to prove. The club helps them get out of the holes they crawl out of—and I do mean holes. People with the brains, the looks, but no future in front of them. The Heritage paves their way to success.

Their debts are paid, their pasts are wiped clean, they get to attend the best schools, and they're a shoo-in for whatever job they want, like Harry."

"Harry Voss?"

Jason nods. "He came out of foster care with nothing but a debt to the dealer he was working for and a target on his back. Now, he's on top of the world. After his year as a thorn, we'd smoothed things out with his past. He went through his initiation, and came out a fucking rock star. Plenty of people find the reward worth it." He grins. "And many like the initiation. It's just one night. Before and after that, they choose who to play with."

I can imagine that if some guy who looks like Jason Alden found girls at rock bottom and asked them if she'd be willing to be tied up and fucked for one night in exchange for all of her wishes to become true, ninety-nine percent of them wouldn't even hesitate.

"So, how am I different?"

"You don't need help. You're not a recruit. When you join the Heritage, you'll be a full member."

"Just like that?"

He tilts his head. "Well, not *just* like that. But after you're an Alden? Certainly."

CHAPTER TWENTY-NINE

Jason

My pretty doll is so cute when she's speechless.

"You did propose this morning," I remind her. "And I said yes."

"I was joking, Jason."

I'm aware. "I wasn't. Come on, Nadia. You knew this was coming." There's no other path for her and me. Our future was written in stone the moment she claimed me all these years ago.

"We've been together for weeks. We're not getting married."

So cute. "Of course we are. I imagine you won't want to live at my parents' next year, and I certainly don't want to commute from Brooklyn, so we're getting a place together. It makes sense to have the wedding before the move. Your parents will feel better."

And the Butcher isn't going to let me live long if he

thinks I'm toying with his daughter. Tying the knot sooner rather than later makes sense for many reasons, chief among them, my survival.

"Jason..."

"Nadia." I get into her bath tub and sigh in contentment. "You coming in? We don't have much time, David's waiting to bring us back to town."

"If we don't have much time, I'm not getting in the bath with you," she says dryly.

"Good point."

"I'm still not marrying you anytime soon. It'd be insane. We're eighteen."

"Nothing between us is even remotely sane, doll. And I'm nineteen."

"What?" She seems confused. "Since when?"

She's going to feel bad, and I don't like it, but there's no helping it. "Yesterday, actually. Well, kind of. I was born on the twenty-nineth of February, which is inconvenient as fuck. Though this year, the month stops at twenty-eight, I'm definitely nineteen now."

I watch as her confusion morphs into anger in front of my eyes. "Why the hell didn't you tell me it was your birthday? I would have done something. A cake, some presents, a party..."

"We had a party," I remind her. "And I had tons of fun, doll, for the first time in years." I don't usually celebrate my birthday , but yesterday, it almost felt like I did.

Understanding hits her, and now she's sad. "It's because of your brother, right? It's also his birthday."

I don't need to confirm she's correct. It's obvious.

She must sense I don't want to dwell on the subject because she continues, "Well, eighteen *or* nineteen is a stupid age to get married. We'll become a statistic. No one stays with their high school sweetheart for more than a few years."

"You'll find the statistic of high school sweethearts who fuck each others' brains out and exchange partners as much as they want highly different, doll. Come on. Since when have I cared what anyone thinks of me?"

"Maybe I care," she mutters.

I stare into her eyes and grin.

"No. This isn't something you get to bully me into. I have to stand there and say 'I do,' you know. And I don't."

She's so funny. "Do you really want me to make you? You know I can." At her defiant stare, I continue. "Let's play this out. I'll come for your father's restaurant first. He's the most vulnerable. Maybe it gets closed because of health code issues." I wrinkle my nose. "Rats. They're pretty disgusting. If he clears things up, his clientele will still have evaporated by the time he can open up again. Then your mother. I can release a sex tape—one of many, I assure you. She'll lose most of her well-to-do friends. Not that they'd mind it, of course. They'll watch it and wank to her moans, but appearances are everything to the likes of them."

"Oh, fuck you, Jason.

"Then, your friends. Not Mel, of course, but your nice

New York crew. I'm not certain what dirt I'll find, but my PI will have a folder in my inbox within the hour."

"Do you have to be an asshole all your life?"

I like the fact that she's no longer afraid of me. Oh, she believes I'd do all that and more to get what I want, and she's right to. I would. But she's not afraid because she knows she'll give in. She wants to be forced, to pretend she can't help her situation, from time to time. I pin her with my look. "Do you want to marry me?"

"Right now, I don't even want to see you, you jerk." She crosses her arms and moves to her closet, dragging her suitcase along.

I chuckle. She ought to know I won't let the conversation end here. "I'm not talking about age or timing or whatever other irrelevant concern you might have. Do you want to become my wife, spend your life with me on your team, by your side, fighting your battles and fucking you until we both die?"

She ignores me, packing away her clothing.

"Do I have to push for an answer? I will."

"Yes, you dick. Someday, when it's appropriate, I probably wouldn't mind..."

"Fuck appropriate. You want to marry me, I want to marry you. No one is going to judge you or question you, Nadia. You're going to be an Alden. All you'll get is the respect you're due."

"They'll call me a gold digger and say I'm probably knocked up," she counters.

I grin. "Not to your face."

"Not to *your* face. People don't mind saying that to me. Look at Christoph."

I have to deal with Billington, and soon. I know the creep has mommy issues and doesn't respect anyone who wasn't born with a seven-figure trust fund, but if he doesn't keep his shit together in front of Nadia, we'll have problems.

"Not to mention, you still don't have any idea who wanted to hurt me last semester."

Ah, that. She hasn't mentioned it in a while, and I'd hoped the concern might have disappeared after weeks of quiet. Apparently, her fear's still there, festering in the background.

And she's very right to be afraid.

"Who said I had no idea?"

She jumps to attention. "What do you mean? You know who was after me? Who was it? Why didn't you tell me?" Her hysteria worsens with every probing question.

I consider my words carefully. "I'm ninety-nine percent certain I know who's behind the fire—and the cat, too." I pause. "And I haven't told you because it's a sensitive matter."

Hiring Lucas was smart. The guy is an annoying shit-head, but he also happens to be a genius. One week scanning through the school security recordings, and he had a clear idea.

"A sensitive matter?" she repeats, yelling. "They tried to kill me!"

"And they will pay for it, when that ninety-nine goes

up to a hundred." I can't afford a miss, given who my target is. "But look, you're safe. We've openly been together for weeks and nothing's happened to you, right?"

I don't tell her the guards found a squirrel with its neck snapped in her gym locker, or that one of her uniforms had been stabbed multiple times.

The psycho can't get anywhere near her, and that's the main thing.

"Jason, you need to tell me what's going on."

The thing with Nadia is, she's not like me. She can't hide her hatred, her suspicion, her ire. Her gorgeous eyes are an open book.

So... "No."

CHAPTER THIRTY

It's been three days and I still want to strangle my boyfriend.

I'm enjoying the holiday break. It's nice to be back at the restaurant and see my friends every day. My parents are both busy, but I have lunch with Uncle Lucius and Lucas on Sunday, and I skate at the ramp with Heather and Gabriella on Monday.

When I get back home, the object of my many murder fantasies is sitting on my bed. "What are you doing here?" I seethe.

He's sent me several texts since our silent ride back to the city, and I've ignored every single one.

"Your mom let me in."

That's not an answer and he knows it.

"Unless you tell me who tried to hurt me, I don't have anything to say to you."

He sighs. "I let you pout for the entire weekend, and most of Monday, doll. Enough now."

I hold the door wide open. "Get out."

Jason remains on my bed.

"I'm not kidding."

"I can see that. Somehow, you seem to have forgotten how it goes. I have all the power, and you have exactly how much I want to give you." He licks his lips. "I love seeing you worked up like that. Makes me hard. I wish we had time to act on it."

"You're in a hurry? Great. *Get out*."

"Sure. Just as soon as you pack and come with me."

"Jason, this is my limit, all right? My safety isn't a toy you can play with."

"Of course not. Which is why I make sure you're perfectly safe."

He's driving me insane.

I can't deny that nothing has occurred since we've been back together, so whatever he's doing to protect me could well be working, but I have the right to know who set my room on fire and *killed a cat* I liked. "Jason..."

"Let's play this out. I tell you what you want to know. You get angry. You confront them, say something that suggests you're aware of their actions, or so much as look at them weird. They notice. They flip. It could happen in the hallway, where your bodyguards can't reach you fast enough, or in a class where none of us are with you. It could happen in the toilet, in the courtyard. Suddenly you have a knife to your throat and you fucking die." He smiles pleasantly. "I'm not taking that chance, doll. It's not my fault you have a terrible poker face."

Some of my anger disappears, because he's not wrong. I can hold my head high and pretend the world doesn't get to me, but when I'm pissed at someone, they know it.

He lifts his chin. "You can come voluntarily, or I can kidnap you. Either way, we're going to Aspen."

"Aspen," I repeat. "Why would we go to Aspen?"

"Because I'm a man of my word. I told you I'd take you to see fresh snow from the mountains." He smiles. "You'll love it."

———

He was right, damn him. The view is breathtaking. Picturesque chalets nestle in a gorgeous mountain town surrounded by snowy peaks. I stay glued to the window during the entire uphill ride. "This is incredible."

"You'll love the cabin. It's just a little higher up, closer to the slopes."

Of course it is. I can count on the Aldens to always have the best positions. I'm sure at the sea, their place is right on the beach, and they probably stay in a castle if they travel to France.

The higher we drive, the more luxurious the cabins become. David parks in front of rustic wooden house with a large porch.

The lights are already on, and I spot figures seated around an outdoor fire.

"It looks like the parents already made it."

"Your parents!" I'm stunned. "You never said anything about meeting your parents."

I look down at what I'm wearing—my red duffle coat as it's the warmest thing I own, jeans, and a white sweater. I've looked worse, but I would have appreciated a warning.

"Don't fuss, they love you."

I sincerely doubt that. There's nothing in me that the likes of Lauren and Charles Alden might love. I'm not well-bred, worldly, I don't have tons of money, and if anything, my family's problematic. "They don't know me."

"They know I love you, and that's enough." He snickers. "I mean, my father would have preferred if I kept the Moores happy, no doubt, but he's fine with you, truly."

Jace climbs out of his car and extends his hand, like he hasn't just dropped several bombs on me.

I'm meeting his parents. His parents approve of me, maybe, sort of? Most importantly...he loves me.

He loves me?

He has the audacity to say those words to me like that, casually, as though they don't matter.

Yet, I'm hardly surprised to hear them. Of course he loves me. I've known that for weeks, if not months.

I take the hand he's holding out to me and follow him to the front door.

A group of forty- or fifty-somethings sit in gilded high-backed chairs set near a firepit right in the patio. Jace brings us over to stand in front of a vacant outdoor couch, but neither of us sits.

I recognize Mr. Alden from all the political campaign ads I've seen, and I don't want to assume who might be his wife, as there are three gorgeous white ladies—and one ebody-skinned one—in their party.

"Mother, Father." Jason gestures to me. "This is Nadia Reyes."

The senator is all smiles. "Call me Charles."

One of the two blondes in the gathering, who looks too young to be his mother, stands and rushes to hug us both. "And I'm Lauren, dear," she gushes. "I was so eager to meet you, darling!"

In my head, she was supposed to secretly hate me and force a smile for Jason's sake, but if she's faking anything, I can't feel it.

Jason and I take our place on the loveseat, and Lauren introduces us to the rest of the party—the Eatons—and after she mentions their name, I do see the resemblance to Maverick—and five other legacy names. I do stare at Viola Billington for longer than I ought to, wondering at her relation to the creep.

"We're on whiskey and cigars, darlings," Lauren tells us. I wonder if she's British, at her use of the endearment, although her accent doesn't betray anything other than upper-class New York. "I know that's not your favorite, what can I serve you?"

Like my parents, they seem rather liberal about alcohol usage, which is hardly surprising, given everything else I know about the couple.

"Do we have any bubbly? Nadia seems quite partial to it, and we have cause to celebrate."

My fingers reach for Jason's thigh and grip it tight in warning.

"Oh? Do tell." Lauren waves her hand and I'm surprised to see Charles get to his feet with an eye roll. He retreats to the kitchen obediently, though.

"Oh, just the start of the winter break. It's Nadia's first time in the mountains, too."

I let go of my hold on his thigh just as his father returns, armed with a bottle in an ice bucket in one hand and a platter of flutes in the other, seemingly comfortable with balancing it all—despite the fact that I can guarantee Charles Alden has never waited tables a day in his life.

"Why are you so stiff?" Jace whispers teasingly. I scowl at him, and he winks, before raising his voice again. "That, and Nadia agreed to marry me."

I'm going to kill him. "I said no such thing!"

"I distinctly remember you saying you'd like to marry me."

"Someday. We're *eighteen*."

"Nineteen, dear," Lauren sees fit to remind me. "My Jace is nineteen."

That literally doesn't make any difference. "Wait, how are you okay with this? Don't you want him to wait, or, I don't know, end up with the girl you chose for him?"

Charles and Lauren exchange a long look. "I may have been hasty and unwise in making a verbal agreement with the Moores when the boys..." Charles catches himself. "When Jason was so young. And obviously, no such agreement is binding."

That's not exactly my point.

"You think?" Maverick's father snorts. "You blue-bloods have no notion of reality."

"You're one to talk, Eaton. Half of your ancestors trace back to the Mayflower," Viola Billington interrupts.

The conversation changes course, as Charles pours us generous flutes of champagne. "Thank you," I say when he hands me mine.

"Anything for my future daughter-in-law." He redirects his attention to his wife, and I turn back to Jason.

"I can't believe you threw me to the wolves."

"Hardly. They don't care, Nadia."

I can believe that now that I've met them.

"My father has old-school ideas, but my mother wears the pants in the relationship," he continues. "And she used to be dirt poor. She doesn't want me to marry for money. What she says goes, in this household."

"Poor?" I gape at him. "You can't be serious." Lauren is the perfect socialite, entirely at ease in this setting.

"Well, the Heritage taught her well." Jason winks.

So, she was one of the club's recruits. After what I've heard of their initiation, I flush.

I've ascended into a different world altogether. Some-place where what I thought I knew doesn't apply.

No wonder I don't quite understand Jason.

CHAPTER THIRTY-ONE

I suck at skiing. In fact, I suck so much I almost break my neck multiple times, but somehow, despite the immediate danger to my life, I'm having a lot of fun.

Jason sticks with me although he's been skiing since before he could walk. He's so comfortable on the snow, zooming backwards and forwards and sideways around me. In almost all things, his level so far above mine it's not even funny. Even so, he seems to be having a good time just teaching me how to slide along the slopes like a penguin, holding my hand when the incline is sharper than I'm comfortable with. We spend the whole morning laughing and goofing around in the crisp fresh air. Although it's sunny, I don't think I've ever been this cold in my entire life.

Jason bought me exorbitant but appropriate mountain gear at the sporting goods store where I was fitted for skis. He wanted to buy those, too, but I convinced him we should just rent them. We're only here for a few days.

The Aldens aren't "renting people", according to his grumbles, but he let me win this one.

It's nice. Spending time with Jason, just me and him, away from Cross and Roses, the craziness of the city, and potential psychos wanting to hurt me.

After hours of exercise, I'm more than happy to settle in at the cabin for a warm hot chocolate spiked with rum, and enjoy the outdoor jacuzzi. After lunch, I tell Jason to join his parents for a real exercise session on the slopes, but he is more than happy to stick with me and get his endurance exercise in the bed instead.

I get some time to catch up on a novel I'd meant to read, and Jason works remotely on a club issue. I hear something about bringing in a new DJ, an acrobat, and a trendy brand of gin. His tone is so professional when he talks over the phone, I doubt his interlocutors imagine that they're dealing with an eighteen-year-old. Although to be fair, who doesn't know Jason Alden these days?

The first night, I'm horrified when I hear the bed above our ceiling squeak, with the sound of muffled moans. "What the hell?"

"That would be my parents."

"Oh my god, aren't you mortified?"

Imagining Mr. and Mrs. Alden going at it like monkeys, I want to hide, and they're not even my parents.

"Hardly," he chuckles, because of course, he's Jason

Alden, above such things as shame. "It's a given they fuck, or I wouldn't be here. Don't you hear your parents go at it?"

"Never." Thank fuck.

This somehow makes him laugh harder. "Someday, you should ask them why."

"Right. My parents. I'll just go up to them and ask, 'so, why aren't you guys screwing?' I should also check what their favorite positions are while I'm at it."

Jason only grins.

The rest of the week passes in a blur of similar activities, skiing, drinking, eating, and fucking, awkward as it might be while we share the house with several adult couples. But Jason doesn't seem to care and I get used to it.

Before I know it, we drive back down the hill, away from the fairy-tale retreat, and head back to the airport. On the way in, we flew first class, which, needless to say, is a first for me. On the way back, we travel in the Alden Corp jet with Lauren—Charles has been called away to DC, and she made him fly commercial.

The inside of the small jet has a luxury lounge bar in cream and oak. Our flight attendants, two well-dressed, handsome men, consider it their mission in life to ensure our flutes are never empty. I could get used to this.

Jason drops me off back at my house for the last night before the end of the break, stopping only long enough to meet my mother.

My father is, as always, working.

Before I know it, we're back at school again.

Either because of the lack of incidents, Jason's assurance that he's seen to my safety, or both, I relax. I don't even ask him who he thinks was behind the fire more than once a week.

The second week of March, the entire senior year is abuzz with energy, talking nonstop about the European trips. I remember to submit my absence papers at the front desk, only to find a confused secretary staring at her computer. "You're not going to Rome? Has there been a change of plans? This close to the date, I'm afraid we might not be able to process a refund as the tickets, hotel rooms, and restaurants have already been booked."

A refund? "I haven't paid for the trip...have I?"

I'm quite certain I haven't, but as I stare at the manicured lady in full makeup, I realize that it's quite possible the payment was made for me without my knowledge.

"We have your full payment recorded...a week ago, isn't that right?"

I vaguely remember talking about the travel to Jason around then. "I don't like the idea of you in Rome without me," he'd said.

Though fluent in French and Italian, Jason takes Spanish and German, so he's headed to Germany.

"Don't worry about that, I'm not going anywhere."

"Why?"

Of course, he'd be confused, he who has never had to check a price tag in his life. "Because it's expensive as fuck. I didn't ask my parents for the money. It doesn't matter, really. If I want to see Rome someday, I'll save up and go for a tenth of the price of that excursion."

I should have expected him to pay for it, but I didn't, mostly because I didn't think he'd want me alone in a foreign country with classmates whose intentions we might not be certain about.

Jason will never cease surprising me.

"That's right," I tell the receptionist. "Sorry for the confusion. I'm going to Rome."

Apparently.

CHAPTER THIRTY-TWO

I'm busy, between classes, resuming swimming, working on my series for the Black and White gallery, and Jason. Always Jason.

Winter recedes reluctantly, giving way to the first warm, sunny days. The Wednesday before my trip to Rome, my art teacher takes me aside after class. "You've grown in the past three years, Nadia. Your technique and your vision are sharper. I was particularly glad to hear about Tisch. Congratulations."

"Tisch?" I stare at the rail-thin teacher.

His mouth opens and he's quick to apologize. "I'm sorry, I thought you knew. I have an old friend on the admissions committee, and he informed me one of my students had been accepted. You should get the letter any day now."

I grin, excited because it's a dream of mine, though I'll never quite know if I entirely got in on my own merit.

I consider shooting a text to Jason, but instead, I head over to the football field.

I have little appreciation for the sport, and Jason never asks me to attend his games, so I rarely ever see this part of the school. I only have to wait a couple of minutes before the players jog by on the green grass.

Spotting him under his helmet, I rush to him and jump in his arms. "I got in! I'm going to Tisch."

He engulfs me in a bear hug and spins me around. "I knew you would, doll. They had to see you're so fucking talented, they'd be stupid not to take you."

He tears his helmet off to kiss me, ignoring his team-mates' teasing and his coach's glower. "Enough of that, Alden. We have a game to prepare for."

Jason keeps kissing me until he's good and ready to let go. "Let's eat out tonight to celebrate. Restaurant in town at six thirty?"

I nod eagerly, and let him get back to his testosterone-infused fun.

When I head back to the front of the U, Jason's car with David isn't waiting for me. I guess since I didn't show up when I usually do, he drove back to Glass. I consider sending him a text, but it's warm and I don't mind the walk.

It's silly to leave the building just to come back for swimming an hour later, but I've gotten used to heading back to the dorms to get changed and chat with Melina.

I'm not the only one walking back, though the

handful of groups I see are heading to the common dorms. I see them take a left to cross the fields, while I have to walk through an orchard to make my way to the lake.

Alone between the rows of apple trees, I start to feel uneasy and glance over my shoulder, hearing a noise.

Suddenly my decision to take a stroll seems rather ill advised.

I see nothing but the quiet, short trees not yet in bloom. It must have been an animal of sort, maybe a bird or a rabbit.

I sigh in relief and mutter, "Get your shit together, Nadia."

Turning back to face the direction I'm going in, I yelp, startled, and come to a sudden stop just a couple of feet away from a hard chest. Martin Lee's standing right in front of me, when I had been alone just seconds ago. "Oh, hi." The jock's a friend of Christoph, and a bit of a dick himself, so I'm not exactly comfortable alone with him.

He doesn't move, so I circle him and keep going.

"You know," Martin calls, footfalls trailing mine, "I never noticed you before this year. I should have, though. You look alike."

I don't know what he's talking about. "What?"

"Lucas and you." He jogs to catch up to my swift pace, when I actively try to put as much distance between us as possible. *Great.*

At least, we're approaching my destination: I can see

Glass around the corner. I just need to walk down to the garden leading to the back entrance where the drivers' cars are kept, and I'll be safe.

"We're cousins," I explain.

He laughs. "Not according to my sources, you aren't."

I make a moue and face him. "What are you talking about?"

"You're his kid, aren't you? He didn't want his little princess to ever end up in the crosshairs, so he hid you."

I come to a stop and stare right at Martin.

Oh, shit.

Holy fucking shit, he's right.

Dots I should have connected long ago suddenly make sense. My parents' relationship—or lack thereof. The way my mother never even touches Dad, how she seems so much more comfortable with Lucius. My uncle's interest in me, more vested than that of my actual father.

I'm not Lucius's niece. I'm his daughter. *Of course* I am. I'm not even surprised. Perhaps I willingly closed my eyes and shoved fingers in my ears to avoid looking at the truth in the face. But deep down, I must have known.

I don't like Martin's victorious gaze. "What's it to you?" I demand, not confirming or denying his statement.

There are a handful of people I need to talk to about this *right now*, and Martin Lee isn't one of them.

"Well, Lucius Astrella pretended to consider working for my father. He asked for some information about our business. Then he used it to run the company into the ground." With each word, he walks closer. "My father was arrested for fraud and died in prison, Nadia."

Holy shit.

I would normally offer condolences, but I feel like we're way past platitudes.

Usually, I like to stand my ground against the likes of him, but we're alone in the orchard, and let's face it, he's a six-foot-something bulky baseball player and I weigh maybe one twenty, one hundred thirty pounds.

I push past him, practically jogging toward Glass. He sets off after me with a chuckle. "Oh, I don't think so."

Martin grabs my wrist, and I turn around, draw my fist back, and punch him as hard as I can, hitting right in his face. I miss the nose, but my knuckles sting so I must have hurt him.

"You bitch!" he spits. His grasp is weaker so I snatch my hand back and keep running, faster.

I risk a glance behind me and hit a solid frame. I open my mouth to tell whoever it is to help, but I close it when the stench of a familiar cologne and cigarettes meets my nose.

Christoph Billington.

I understand then.

I've been herded like cattle.

I turn around and start to run, but I'm not fast enough. Christoph grabs me and covers my mouth with some kind of rag. Kicking my legs to get away, I let out a muffled scream and try not to breathe in, but if anything, my frantic fighting and my useless punches only make me breathless and force me to inhale. Slowly, I lose the fight for consciousness.

Everything goes black.

CHAPTER THIRTY-THREE

I wake up, groggy, confused, and nauseous. Everything around me is dark, and my blurred vision isn't the only reason why.

I blink and manage to discern two long legs at eye level.

"There she is, our sleeping beauty. I much prefer them awake, don't you?"

I know that voice, but I can't place it right away.

With some effort, I manage to lift my gaze, and I distinguish Christoph's smug grin.

Fuck. Everything comes back to me in a flash. I recoil, only to find my movements limited. I look down at my feet, and see my ankles are tied to a radiator. We're in a barren room with a small metallic bed, a cheap office chair, and a desk. The only light is from a small office lamp on the empty desk.

"What the hell?"

"Not very bright, is she?" Martin Lee comes out of an adjacent room with a roll of duct tape in hand.

Oh, fuck no.

"Stay away from me."

Both boys laugh. My eyes remain on Christoph, the main threat to me. He's a psycho, and he has made no secret of his intentions towards me.

Shit. I should have called David. I should have stayed safely in the U. By now, I'd be getting ready to go out and celebrate my Tisch acceptance with Jason.

Jason.

Despite the fear buzzing through my blood, I feel a sudden spark of hope. Jason is looking for me already. I know it. He has staff watching me; they would have reported my absence.

Oh, god. Why the fuck did I cut through the orchard instead of walking safely on the road, where anyone could have seen me? I'm a fucking idiot.

"You don't give orders here, pretty girl." Christoph stalks to me, and pressed up against the radiator as I am, there's nowhere to go. I bend to undo the restraints at my ankle and something cold touches my forehead.

I freeze. Christoph is holding a gun against my forehead.

Oh, no.

No, no, no.

They didn't take me to rape me, as I first worried. Martin lost his father and he wants mine to pay for it. He wants to kill me.

"We should just kill her now." Martin says, confirming my fear.

Tears fall along my cheeks. I purposely keep my eyes on Christoph, firstly because he's the one holding the gun, but also because he's my best hope. I don't think he wants to kill me—at least, he doesn't just want to kill me. Chris is obsessed with fucking me, probably because I didn't immediately spread my legs when he asked.

I can try to play on that, buy some time. One more second, one minute, maybe an hour.

Jason is going to find me. He is. I have to believe that. "Don't let him hurt me, please," I cry. "Please. I'll do anything, anything."

Christoph's blue eyes light as he smirks. "Anything, hm?" He lowers the barrel to my mouth, pushing it past my lips. "You offering me your pussy, Nadia? Tut, tut. Such a slut. What would your prince charming think?"

Hot humiliation makes me cry harder.

"Come on, Billington, get it over with," Martin seethes.

He considers it and I just sit there, completely still, hoping and hoping these aren't my last seconds. "Nah, I don't think so. I want to play with her first."

Martin scoffs. "That would be downright stupid. There would be DNA proof then."

"Not if I wrap it up. Or we can always come on her and hose her down. Besides," Christoph adds, "there won't be anything left after we dump her in the lake."

They're so fucking casual, I would bet this isn't their

first time hurting...no, *killing* a woman. They've done it before, and they're going to do it to me.

"Fine," Martin allows.

Fuck them. Fuck them both.

My eyes are still shut, but I can hear Christoph unzipping his pants. He removes the gun out of my mouth, only to replace it with something just as thin and short: his hard cock.

I want to bite it off.

"Make it good and I'll make sure your last moments don't hurt, pretty girl." He pushes forward, choking me.

Another cock comes into vision, Martin standing next to Christoph. He might have preferred killing me right away, but he isn't against getting his rocks off either.

I take it in my hand, disgusted and so fucking afraid.

Another second, and another one. I just want to survive this, one moment at a time.

Christoph works his way in and out of my mouth, pushing too far and fast. I gargle and slobber all over him, but he doesn't seem to mind. "What a good fucking whore you are. Alden trained you well. You would have made out like a queen in the Heritage if you'd only known your fucking place." Each word is punctuated with more assault. Christoph finishes in my mouth and get to his knees, putting the gun down to spread my thighs.

Even though everything in me wants me to fight back, I don't. I do nothing. I can't risk him changing his mind and pulling the trigger. This is all about survival.

How can I survive? Not by waiting for a prince charming, that's for sure. I trust Jason *is* looking for me. I just don't know how long he'll take and I can't afford to wait.

I glance at the gun and close my eyes, still pumping Martin's disgusting member. My other hand is free. It's not that far, and Christoph is too busy tearing my clothes off to pay attention to it.

He'll have to undo my bonds on at least one leg, if he wants to fuck me—I can almost feel it.

I wait patiently, letting him touch me, lowering his mouth to me to try to get me wet. When he doesn't manage to, he spits on his condom-covered small cock and presents it at my entrance. The angle isn't working, and with both of my legs bound, he can't move me much. As I expect him to, he takes the knife from his back pocket and cuts off the rope between my feet, just as Martin tries to press his cock against my mouth.

I bite down hard. "What the fuck! Bitch." Martin slaps my face, but I don't even let the pain register.

I wrap my bare legs around Christoph to keep him in position, like my martial arts teacher showed me a decade ago, and then I sink my teeth into his nose, biting so hard that he bleeds. He screams and tries to get free, but I keep my position firm and grab the gun. I point it at Christoph first, remove the safety, and shoot without hesitation.

Martin pulls a piece concealed in his back pocket and points it at me just as I redirect the barrel toward him.

His eyes are so full of hatred, I know there's a chance he'll take the shot even if it guarantees I'll shoot too.

We're about to die together, unless I can talk him down. The likelihood of managing that is low. Christoph was a sexist creep who considered himself entitled to me, to women in general. Proving him right was easy. Martin just wants blood.

And he gets it.

The deafening sound of a gun firing takes both of us by surprise. Blood pools out of his chest, staining his white shirt right over his heart. As life leaves him, Martin Lee takes one last shot.

His hand lowers millimeters, and I move as much as I can in the fraction of a second.

I scream, blinding pain seizing me. I would pass out if not for the adrenaline pumping through my veins.

I see Martin fall flat on the ground. I didn't even hear the thud. My ears are still ringing, have been ringing since I fired the first shot.

My stomach's all twisted into knots, and I think I'm going to be sick, for various reasons. My entire body is trembling, shaking.

"You're all right, doll. Everything is going to be all right."

Jason. He came. He's here.

His arms envelop me, and I cry, and cry, and cry.

"Her clothes. Why is she...*fuck*. They hurt her. They fucking hurt her." I'd recognize that voice anywhere.

I lift my eyes to Lucas as Jason removes his letter jacket and puts it on my shoulders, covering me to mid-thigh.

Lucas holds a gun in his hand. He's the one who shot Martin. Who saved my life. "You're my brother," I tell him, half delirious with the pain of my shoulder.

"We need to call an ambulance. And the cops." Cain. He walks in and look down at the corpses bleeding on the floor. "Especially the cops."

I laugh against Jason's chest.

I want to vomit and I've never felt this much pain, not even after the burns, but I laugh anyway. I'm alive.

CHAPTER THIRTY-FOUR

I f I never see a sterile care room again, it'll be too soon.

The school ambulance takes me to a clinic owned by the Heritage. Because of course, they have clinics. The cops take my vague, simplified statement on the night of the event, and the next day, I have to recount the entire story again in front of a different audience.

I don't omit a single detail. I let the board of the Heritage know exactly what happened with their sick members. Jason's father takes the shoulder that wasn't shot and squeezes it. "We will demand reparations from the Billingtons and the Lees for what happened to my son's fiancée," he warns, sternly.

"Reparations?" Viola sniffles. "She killed my boy."

"Your boy raped her, and intended to do worse," Charles snarls. "This isn't over. Not by a long shot."

In Jace's bed, I alternate between sleeping and crying

for a whole week. Overall, things could have been much worse. I might have been hurt a little physically, but I'm still in one piece. The only permanent damage will be the scar of the gunshot wound.

I'm still a mess. There's bullying, and then there's this shit. Fuck Christoph. Fuck Martin.

Jason doesn't leave me alone, not for one moment. He even sits in front of the bathroom while I pee.

What he doesn't do is touch me.

It takes me days to ask, "How long have you known he wanted to...?"

"I didn't," Jason. "I swear I didn't. Chris was... Shit, Nadia, he wasn't even on my radar. I thought it was someone else entirely." He seems disgusted with himself.

I reach out for his hand and squeeze it.

He found me.

I wake up about ten days later without crying, and I don't cry for the rest of the day. I'm grateful I seem to have shed all my tears. Light from the far wall almost blinds me. The curtains have been pushed back from the window. Early morning light filters through the glass, and I know there won't be any more sleep for me.

I roll over to look at Jason, who's awake again. I wonder if he slept at all in the last week. "Who did you think it was?"

"Sorry?"

"You said you didn't suspect Christoph. Who did you think might be after me?" The question comes out a whisper, as though I'm afraid to summon ghosts.

"Yuki."

I blink, gaping at him as I slowly sit up.

"She's not one to let go of her toys. All the pieces fit. On camera, she's talking to Marie Vaughn the day she destroyed your sculpture, she chats with staff in the faculty building—people who might have access to camera recordings. We see her charm a janitor in your old dorm—and janitors are not her style. She's dangerous, and the Moores have almost as many resources as us. I had eyes on her at all times." He shakes his head. "I'm sorry I wasn't more diligent, faster."

"It wasn't your fault a couple of psychos wanted to hurt me." It kills me that he feels so guilty. I'd first assumed that the psycho were after me because of him, when the vendetta had been about my family. "And you were just in time. You *saved* me."

Him and Lucas. My brother.

He came to see me at the hospital the first day, but I haven't seen him since. I'll have to, and soon. We have a lot to talk about. And I need to hug him for at least a century for killing Martin before he could pull the trigger when the gun was aimed at my head.

I shift to be on my knees, release Jason's hand so that I can grip his face with both of mine, and plant a kiss on his lips. Groaning against him, I lick his lips, pushing hard enough that he knows to open his mouth. My tongue sweeps inside.

I need this, need to forget the bitter taste of the two boys who tried to destroy me.

Jace grunts into my mouth, breaks off the kiss, and tilts his head forward, touching his forehead to mine. Without moving away, I look up to see a serious expression on his face. "I figured you wouldn't want to...you know. After that."

He's talking about Martin and Chris. I understand the assumption. They didn't even force themselves on me, I offered to fuck them to survive. What he doesn't understand is that I need him *because* of them. "You don't need to treat me like porcelain."

"You were raped by two guys who wanted to kill you."

I shake my head. "It could have been much worse. And I got a good bite in," I manage to joke. "That was pretty awesome."

Jason doesn't seem to see the funny side. "You need time."

He's unbearable. "Stop being bossy and telling me what you think I need. I want your cock in my mouth because it's hard and big and gorgeous and *mine*." I climb into his lap and rub against him. "I want you because you're my choice. I want to want it with someone I trust, someone I love."

My hands fumble to remove his clothes and he lets me undo his zipper, grabbing his cock.

My kisses are punishing, hard and fierce, like I want to claim Jace as my own, leave my mark on him. My hands rub up and down his back as I shed my own clothing. He watches, not pushing to take control for once. Biting my lip, I climb over his cock and lower myself on it, burying it deep.

Jace rumbles and throws his head back, letting me ride him fast and hard, taking more and more and more, climbing toward the inevitable cliff.

My nails rake up and down his back, hard enough to leave scratches. Jason starts to fuck me from underneath as I ride him harder.

"More," I gasp out.

His hand gets to my clit and start rubbing it furiously. I jerk as if struck by lightning. His fingers are magic, and I continue to rock on top of him, meeting his upward thrusts. I'm so close, so close... And then I scream right along with him. He shudders, emptying himself inside me.

I kiss his jaw, below his ear, and then his lips.

I should be sated, but I'm not, not even close. I want him again. And again. And again.

Today and every day until our last breaths.

EPILOGUE

I wake up to a mouth against my clit and I grin, glancing down. Instead of the blond, wavy hair I get every day, the man between my legs has longer, silky brown hair. He lifts his icy blue eyes to me and grins.

"Cain," I giggle, unsurprised.

It's hardly the first time he and his girlfriend have snuck into our bed since Jason gave them a spare key to our new apartment. They come whenever they feel like it. I guessed they'd feel like it today.

"Hey, cupcake."

Next to me, Jason's growling against the fold of the blonde who's sitting on his face.

I didn't understand why Jason was so adamant to leave Cain out of our sex life for years, when he's more than happy to play with most of his friends and acquaintances, even if I never pushed him for an answer. I get it now, though.

Cain and Jason were already close—brothers, more than friends—before we started to play together. Now, it's almost as if the four of us are in a relationship together. If we'd crossed that line before he found someone to love and understand him, we might have ended up as a throuple.

I like things as they are. Although Cain has got to stop waking us up at dawn on Sundays.

Panting, I reach out to grasp Jason's dick as Cain's expert tongue teases my folds. He grunts between her legs, his hips thrusting into my hand.

Keeping my legs parted, knees on either side of Cain's face, I bend forward and lower my face to Jason's cock.

Cain gets to his knees and directs his thickness at my entrance, plunging in without having to ask if I want him. He knows I do.

The four of us writhe, moan and scream each other's names for at least an hour.

"Thanks for that," Cain rasps. "I'm going to need it if I have to deal with my father again."

Cain hasn't seen his father for years, but today will be an exception.

Jason wanted Cain's mother to be present for our wedding, and Cain's mother doesn't go anywhere without his father.

"Ready to get hitched?" he asks, wiping his cum from my naked stomach.

Delaying our wedding until Jason and I finished college is my greatest accomplishment. If he'd had his way, we would have been married five years ago. I'm glad I managed to make him wait.

I've made a mark in this world as me, Nadia Astrella, daughter of a vaguely honest businessman and a ballerina, niece of a gay workaholic who loved me enough to claim me when I was vulnerable. I have a website where I sell my art for thousands, and occasionally, it shows in galleries—though I never let Jason talk to any owner about me again.

Now I'm ready to become his in every humanly possible way, including adding another ring to the gorgeous square diamond on my left hand.

I glance at the man buried inside one of my best friends, diving into her with harsh, punishing thrusts.

"Am I ever."

The End

Emm writes under three pen names and prioritizes which series to work on by looking at the number of reviews, so if you enjoyed *Spin the Damn Bottle* and would like to get the next in *All The Games We Play* soon, don't forget to leave a few words!

Next in the series: *Seven Minutes in Hell* (a standalone.)

For updates, teasers and more, join Emm's Facebook group or follow her.

Stay tuned for an excerpt of *Suck it Up*, Willow's sister's dark story.

Two years ago, the protective big brother who spoiled me was murdered, and everyone I know thinks he deserves it. If losing Chris isn't enough, Rowan White has decided to make me pay for his alleged sins.

I can't believe Chris would really hurt anyone, but when I looked for answers, all I got was punishment.

I did everything to stay away from the golden prince's wrath. I gave up my place at Harvard just to avoid him.

My shitty luck strikes again, because the devil is back in town, and he's not done with me.

SUCK IT UP

I need a new job before I murder my boss.

Silks was never the most upstanding of strip clubs to begin with. Plenty of the girls dancing and serving here are happy to go into private rooms and work on their backs for a hundred bucks, but when Vinnie was in charge, the rest of us felt protected. If we wanted to, we kept our masks on, earned our tips, then were free to go home.

Bernard, the new sleaze in charge, has other ideas.

"No." You'd think that word is simple enough for his diminutive brain. One syllable. Most toddlers understand it.

"They're offering a lot of money to talk to you privately. Just a talk, mind, and it's a grand," he says, completely ignoring me.

I suppose his attention is too focused on my exposed tits for him to hear me. Some guys just can't multitask. I pull my hoodie over my head, covering the cupless silver bra. Maybe that'll get help him concentrate on my actual words.

"I don't dance. I don't do private *talks*. And I sure as fuck don't do it for a thousand dollars." No one would offer that much cash without expecting to get their dick very, very wet.

I'm not a prostitute. I wait tables in this strip joint because I make over a hundred bucks per night in tips and I have bills to pay. I just graduated from high school, but for the last few years, I've had very little time to work between my classes and the fact that I'm, for all intents and purposes, my little sister's parent. Mom's still around, but only when she's passed out. As soon as she wakes up, she gets out of doors to rush to the MC hang-out where she can get her fill of drugs, alcohol, and cocks.

I'm only free at night. There isn't much else I *can* do except work at a gas station, and that wouldn't cover a tenth of my expenses.

I actually used to like my job before Bernard bought this place. Watching the insanely talented women dance on the poles is fun. Sure, some clients get a little grabby, but Vinnie's bouncers used to stop them the moment they put their hands on us. Now, I'm on my own when someone wants to cop a feel.

I don't judge the girls here who screw their clients. My

closest friend, Lola, started fucking for cash when she was sixteen because she couldn't find a job, with her baby face and her two left feet. Among my fellow waitresses, I know that Marina has two kids with special needs. You wouldn't believe her hospital bills. If taking limp dicks helps her stay afloat, good for her. I just don't want to fuck strangers for money. In fact, I don't think I want to fuck at all. Sex can lead to children, and I already have one—a sixteen-year-old, barely three years younger than me. I'm tired, broke, and bitter. Let's not add pregnant to that glowing resume.

"Listen here, Morgan." Bernard crosses his arms on his chest. "You work for me. If I say you gotta talk to those clients, you gotta talk to them."

I stare at his double chin for a moment, fantasizing about punching his carotid artery. Or I could be boring and just go for his junk. "Fine."

His flushed face starts to morph into a leering grin.

I open my locker up again, to clean out the few personal possessions I keep here: a deodorant, my portable phone charger, and some spare change. "I guess I quit."

I can't afford to, but quitting was always the plan. Graduation was a week ago. I can apply for a day job now. It'll be nice for Willow to have someone there at night. Not to mention, safe. I stress out about leaving her alone in our trailer. Some of our neighbors are all right, like Lola's family. I know her little brothers would help

Willow if something happens. But there are also dodgy guys who openly ogle us like they aren't three times our age, waiting for the first hint of vulnerability to pounce. I've seen it happen to Lola. Her family was a month late on rent and about to get kicked out when Mr. Dwight offered her some spare cash for "helping out around the house." And now Lola's gone.

Seven weeks. A month and a half. She disappeared mid-April and it's the first week of June. There's no trace of her online, and Lola was a social media addict.

Is. She *is* a social media addict. She's alive. She's all right. I have to believe that.

I don't ever want Willow to fall into that void. She's too bright, too sweet, and she's mine to protect.

"Wait a minute…"

I walk out of the changing room. "You can mail me my last check."

I know I'll never see that check, but at least I got decent tips today.

Bernard snatches my wrist, holding me back. "You're going to speak to them, you bitch."

Fuck this.

I spit in his face and stomp on his foot with my four-inch heels. He yells and lets go of me. I still punch his nose, though. I'm not gonna lie: it's satisfying.

Making sure my hood's low over my eyes, I leave Silks behind for good.

I was very careful to conceal my employment. Thorn

Falls might be a larger town, but rumors run rampant if left unchecked, and I can't afford a reputation. Lola has one, and I've seen her brothers get into so many fights because of it. I don't give a shit about what the people here think of me, but I didn't want my job to haunt Willow's footsteps.

I walk to my rusty bicycle, unlock it, and ride home, a weight lifted off my shoulders. It's done. I don't work at Silks anymore. I'm free.

Finding a new job isn't going to be easy in this town, especially since I don't have a reference. I never intended to use a reference from Silks, and no one expect eighteen-year-olds to come with years of previous employment, so punching Bernard is inconsequential.

I should try the florist. My friend Erica used to work there, up until she got engaged to one of the biggest wallets in town. I didn't try to get her job when she quit in January because Silks paid a lot better, and her boss only offered her about two hours of work per day. Still, considering my bank balance, I can't afford to be choosy. Maybe they still need help.

Thorn Falls is situated in a cluster of hills, which is picturesque, except when you're cycling up to reach the trailer park. My place's at the very end of the west side, as far away from the gaudy McMansions of the riverside as possible. That way, the wealthy folk can forget people like me exist.

I notice the sound of the sirens before I see the

strobing police lights. I speed up, my heart heavy in my chest. It definitely sounds like it's coming from the trailer park.

I try to reason with myself. If there is an issue, it could be at any of the twenty-something trailers of Bellerive Park. It doesn't have to be mine. Willow's fine. She is. There's no other alternative.

And yet, when I arrive, the three police cars are parked right in front of our trailer. Willow's in the back of one of their cars.

Along with my mother.

"What's going on?" I cry, dropping my bike to rush to my sister.

A burly man in uniform blocks my path. "Miss, we are in the middle of an investigation."

What the fuck? "That's my sister in there," I retort. "She's a minor. You can't do this. She didn't do anything."

Willow's a bookworm whose biggest offense is reading entire trilogies in one night.

"Are you Ms. Brown? Morgan Brown?"

My stomach sinks. Why does he know my name? They could be here for me. That doesn't explain what Willow and our mother are doing in the back of the car, though.

I remember thinking every police raid was meant for me for years. Then, one day, they came for my father. He was locked up for dealing three years ago, and since then, I've stayed far away from shit that could get me in trouble. I commit one offense: working under someone else's name. I used Lola's ID because she was eighteen back when I applied at Silks. We don't really look alike; she has blue eyes, mine are green. I'm blonde and she dyes her hair pink. Vinnie didn't spare more than a glance for the ID, so it worked.

"Why?" I stall, reluctant to confirm my identity without more information.

"You'd better come to the station." The man takes my arm and leads me to the back of a different cruiser than the one my mother and sister are locked inside.

What is it tonight with me who think they can touch me? "Let go of me!" I pull my arm back. "Am I under arrest?"

His brows knit. "No, Ms. Brown, but your mother is. As Ms. Willow Brown is underage, she might have to stay with a foster family for a time..."

No fucking way. "I can look after Willow." I have for the last few years. "I'm eighteen."

The policeman sends me a condescending look. I want to hit something. That's not likely to help, so I just get into the car, seething.

What is going on?

I'm relieved the police cars are on the move shortly after. My mind runs at a thousand miles a minute, trying to guess what my mother could have done. Soliciting? Possible. Stealing? Likely.

Fuck. How can I fix this?

We park at the back of the station and they usher me inside like I'm a criminal. "Where's my sister?" I demand.

"Taken care of."

I don't like his tone. I don't like anything about the situation at all. It's eleven at night, Willow was dragged out of the trailer—out of her bed, most likely—and I can't even see her.

Fists tight, I attempt to control my anger. Willow might be the one with our grandmother's red hair, but I inherited the temper. I know losing it isn't going to help me with these assholes though. They'd love a reason to lock me up right next to my mother. The west side kids have always been trash in the eyes of the law.

"After you," the policeman says, opening a door to a sterile gray office that looks like an interrogation room from shitty TV show.

"I'm not going anywhere until I know where my sister is."

"On her way to New York."

I recognize that voice. I've heard it before, though I can't place it. It's not the kind of voice you forget. It's low and as smooth as chocolate.

Where have I heard it before?

I step toward the direction of the voice, into the room, and stop dead in front of him.

Six-foot-four of tanned, lean muscles, dirty blond, silky hair, piercing blue eyes and a pouty mouth made of sin.

Camden Hunt, the prince of Thorn Fall.

Out of all of the rich assholes in this town, his father is the worst.

In the past, I wouldn't ever have been allowed within ten yards of His Majesty, but since Erica landed one of his best friends, I've seen him a couple of times. He even danced with me once at the wedding. I told him I couldn't waltz. He asked if I could shut the hell up and follow.

"What did you just say?"

He didn't just tell me my sister's going to New York, because that makes no sense at all.

"And here I thought you were supposed to be smart." He pushes up from the wall against which he'd been leaning, and takes one step toward me. "I said Willow's going to the airport. By the time she lands, I'll text her social worker the address where she's supposed to go. Mr. and Mrs. Crawford of Fifth Avenue feel quite lonely now that their wonderful two-point-three children have flown the nest. They'll spoil her rotten. Or, I could send her to the Martins. Trust me when I tell you that they make your parents look like angels."

My eyes widen. He can't mean that, right? "Are you threatening my sister?"

"Of course not. I'm threatening you." Camden tilts his head. "Sit."

Preorder Now
Or join Emm's group for news about special editions with bonuses

Suck it Up is a *dark* new adult romance entirely unsuitable for sensitive readers. If you thought *Spin the Damn Bottle* was a little much, *Suck it Up* is not for you. If you could go further down the twisted rabbit hole that is the Heritage, jump in!

Printed in Great Britain
by Amazon